I0692296

DESTINATION KOREA

*Navy Seals join forces with a Nuclear attack
submarine to face the threat from North Korea –
a Top Secret mission that employs state of the art
technology while in harm's way.*

BY JACK FREEZE

Printed in the United States.

ISBN 978-1-62806-171-0

Library of Congress Control Number 2018944579

Salt Water Media
29 Broad Street, Suite 104
Berlin, MD 21811
www.saltwatermedia.com

FOREWORD

The present state of affairs in the world today is a result of third world countries that attempt to develop nuclear weapons.

It is certain that a clear and present danger exists with North Korea, a rogue nation controlled by a power hungry and brutal leader.

This novel applies Naval technology to the situation in order to deescalate the seemingly unresolvable standoff by militarily removing the leadership. The conclusion of the story highlights the methods that could be employed to develop North Korea into a strong economic and prosperous nation.

The novel does concentrate on the technical aspects of the mission, such as the capabilities of the nuclear submarine. But, it also includes the personalities of Seals involved in order to show the dedication and skills of the brave men and women who serve.

NAVY HYMN

Eternal Father, strong to save,
Whose arm hath bound the restless wave,
Who bidd'st the mighty ocean deep
Its own appointments limits keep,
Oh, hear us when we cry to Thee,
For those in peril on the sea.

TABLE OF CONTENTS

CHAPTER ONE

"Now Hear This"

New London Naval Base

He stood there in the doorway of the local geedunk while looking for a seat to enjoy his coffee. Petty Officer First Class Tom Burns was an imposing six foot athlete considering the fact that he had three service hash marks on his sleeve. It had been twelve years since Hell Week at the Coronado California Seal Training Center. His Trident badge sat above the four rows of ribbons which included the Navy Cross and Purple Heart with the Parachute Badge following below.

A familiar voice from the past caught his ear and beckoned him over. "Hey Tom, I've got a seat here." It was Chief Petty Officer Jack Cody whom he hadn't seen since taking the advanced communications course at Annapolis.

The Chief also displayed the Trident and Parachute Badge but they had served in different Seal Teams. His commendations included the Distinguished Service Cross and also the Purple Heart.

"It's great to see you Chief. What are you doing here?" as they shook hands.

"I could ask you the same question Tom."

"Well, I'm assigned a billet on the new Virginia Class attack submarine, the USS Richmond that's soon to be commissioned down at Newport News."

"That's fantastic," the Chief replied, "so am I! Then apparently we're both here for the same reason." He adds.

"Yep," Tom explains, "we're both going to have to be qualified in the Submarine Escape Trainer before we embark on our assignment."

"Excuse me," the Master Chief at the next table remarks, "I couldn't help but overhear. I'm the training specialist. Let me give you a heads up. The Escape Trainer consists of an 84,000 gallon pool of water in a 40 foot column. There are two escape trunks to practice on that simulate escape from a downed submarine. The escape trunk on the boat is a small compartment that allows the sailor to transfer between two areas of different pressures. It used to be that he put on the Stenke Hood that was comprised of an inflatable life jacket and a hood to enclose the head. This method replaced the old Momsen Lung that dates back to World War Two. But now the latest is the Mark 11 SEIE Submarine Escape Immersion Equipment and it's included in all Virginia Class submarines. It's a whole body suit that enables free ascent by providing extensive protection for the crewman with a thermal liner to prevent cold

Escape Training Tank
Library of Congress

shock."

"Thanks Chief – Tom, I heard that this system will raise the sailor at a rate of 2 to 3 meters a second and from a depth of 600 feet! Those Brits that designed this thing are pretty sharp."

"Yeah, but we've got to be careful Jack, there's a lot of disqualification due to upper respiratory congestion and middle ear barotrauma."

"Fortunately, Tom, this is the last resort for a submarine rescue. The rescue team always uses the Submarine Rescue Vehicle as the preferred option. It connects directly to a submarine escape hatch to allow the crew members to avoid direct exposure to cold water and high pressure at depth."

"Ha! I'll think of that as I make my ascent, it can't be any worse than free fall at 35,000 feet. Those HALO jumps (high altitude low opening) at minus 50 degrees could cause hypoxia from the low oxygen if you didn't pre-breathe 100 percent oxygen for thirty minutes prior to the jump."

"You're right Tom, this'll be a piece of cake."

Next Morning

"Who wants to go first?" the instructor asks.

"I will," said Jack .

"Ok, climb into this full body buoyancy suit and zip up."

"Got it ? Ok, now climb into the escape chamber and inflate the suit with air. Give me a sign when it's full."

"I will now wrap your legs together with velcro below the knees and tie you to a safety tether."

"Now, seal the door and hold on while the chamber fills with icy water."

While talking through the audio system, the instructor says that the hatch will open and Jack will rise very quickly to the surface. Tom is at the top of the tank and watches Jack shoot up in his red buoyancy suit like a launched missile. As soon as he breaks through the surface, his hip pouch deploys a raft which he bails out and climbs into – then he zips it up to avoid the elements.

"Great job Jack, looks like fun," Tom shouts while laughing.

"Ok sailor, it's your turn now."

Tom repeats the procedure and later they compare notes.

"It's amazing how fast you rise to the surface," Tom remarks.

"Yes, and to rise in a pressurized suit where you don't get the bends is a real breakthrough," Jack adds.

"I guess we qualify Jack, here's a copy of our orders to report to Norfolk tomorrow."

"Good. Let's get the show on the road."

Norfolk Naval Base

"Good morning Lieutenant, we're here to report to Commander Slater."

"Yes, go right on in, he's expecting you."

"Thank you ma'am."

The two veteran Seals enter the room, salute, and stand at attention. "Sir, I'm Chief Cody and this is Petty Officer Burns, reporting for duty."

"Good, welcome aboard," the Officer replies, "stand at ease."

"I'm the Executive Officer of the soon to be USS Richmond. You are assigned to the Richmond to take part in a mission called Operation Mongoose. It is classified Top Secret so the details of the mission will be disclosed after we have received orders from USPACOM and have been underway for two days out of Pearl Harbor. This is a voluntary mission which you have accepted and I applaud you for that. Meanwhile, you will begin training for the mission prior to the commissioning of the boat next month. Your assignment will include the operation of an underwater vehicle and the disabling of an antidrone radar system."

"You will need to keep your physical skills, weapons expertise, and specialty training at their peak which I know is standard procedure. The training personnel will contact you at 0800 tomorrow. Here's a chit for you to go to the motor pool and get a vehicle to carry you back and forth to Newport News Shipbuilding. You will be billeted here because you will train over at Dam Neck close by with a short trip to Coronado. The Richmond will be at Dry Dock 12. The chief of the boat (COB) will give you an orientation today. Just ignore the welders and electricians as you go through. It's an understood custom to make room as someone passes by even if you are working. See Command Master Chief

Parker when you arrive. Any questions?"

"Good. I will monitor your progress on the special training from time to time. So, keep me posted. Carry on!"

"Aye, aye Sir," Jack responds enthusiastically.

They both salute sharply and depart. As they were leaving, Tom says, "Hey Jack, what's a Mongoose?"

"It's a small fast animal that kills venomous snakes."

Newport News Shipbuilding

Traffic was heavy as they pulled out of the base onto Admiral Taussig Boulevard. "Tom, you know your way around here, don't you?"

"Yes, our home is in Virginia Beach. Mary and the girls are there and I hope to get a couple of weekends off before we depart. Take Route 64 North and go through the Hampton Roads Bridge Tunnel. Then go left on 664 to Newport News – about a half hour run."

Upon arriving, they parked and walked over to Dry Dock 12. "Good grief! She must be longer than a football field," Tom exclaims. Men were everywhere; climbing over the hull, checking equipment, and moving in and out of hatches.

"Hello there! Follow me to Chief Parker's office," a Seaman shouts over the din of the noise.

"Welcome to the Richmond," the grizzled dark skinned Master Chief Parker said. He had so many hash marks on his sleeve that one wonders if he was a retread from World War Two. "I'm the COB, Chief of the

Virginia Class Submarine
Public Domain - US Navy Photo

Boat. It's about the same responsibility as the Master at Arms on surface ships although they focus mainly on law enforcement and weapons control. My job is to get things done, and I do," as he raises his thumb for emphasis. The two Seals certainly believed that!

"We're here for the nickel tour," Jack adds, "we'll be guests for the next deployment. By the way Chief, where are you from, I notice that you're Native American?"

"Yes, and proudly so! I am a direct descendent of Quanah Parker, the famous chief of the Comanches during the late nineteenth century. I'm from Lawton, Oklahoma near Fort Sill – where else, but the reservation."

"I wondered," Jack replied, "I'm from Muskogee."

"It's nice to meet another Sooner," Chief Parker shouts as he walks toward the bow. "Let's start with the exterior of the boat. This is a Virginia Class attack submarine under the newly released Block 111 program. Block 1 and 11 have already been delivered. It has all the latest features and technology for stealth, speed, weaponry, and countermeasures. She cost about $2.7 billion dollars and she's worth it! I don't mean to preach but her capabilities are overwhelming – antisubmarine warfare, antisurface warfare, strike warfare, special ops support, intelligence gathering, surveillance, recon, and mine warfare."

"Notice the rounded bow. It has sonar sensors in it that provide a spherical search. They're called the "Large Aperture Bow (LAB) array, there's a "chin" array under the bow and a conformal array on the sail. This will permit mapping of the ocean floor and location of surface and submerged mines. This system goes all the way around by including side look arrays combined with a towed array to provide quick target location. When deployed, the TB-23 towed array is 900 feet long with 100 hydrophones on a 2500 foot cable. It can detect surface, underwater, and airborne activity, as well as propeller speed."

"The beauty of all these arrays is their ability to transmit on a medium frequency for range information by measuring the time of the return echo or just be passive and not transmit but acquire incoming sonar signals from other sources, primarily the enemy."

"This ship will operate at speeds greater than 25

knots when submerged and be able to dive to 800 feet and beyond – at a 20 degree angle if necessary. These numbers are not classified but the limits are secure."

"She has a low acoustic signature, and stealth capability better than the new Russian Yasen class. Newly designed anechoic coatings on the hull, isolated deck structures, acoustic windows, and composite sonar domes minimize any echo return from enemy sonar signals."

"On the stern, we don't have to go back, there's a duct that surrounds the pumpjet propulsor to mask any cavitation due to the high speed water flow. Tiny air bubbles create noise that is vulnerable to sonar. There's no propeller."

"She'll operate in open ocean and shallow coastal waters – a Littoral environment. She can linger quietly in shallow water. They call it 'fly by wire'. The operator orders depth, speed, and course, then software directs movement of the planes and rudder to maintain the command parameters."

"Let's climb up topside. The things that you need to see are there. In this latest version of Block 111, there are two vertical launch tubes instead of twelve. Each will house six weapons and be called obviously, 'six-shooters'. It's called a Common Weapons Launcher (CWL) and can launch UGM-109 Tomahawk Cruise missiles. The torpedo tubes can launch Harpoon missiles, unmanned aerial vehicles (UAV), and underwater unmanned vehicles (UUV). But also on this mission, we'll launch an aerial intelligent drone (AID)."

"Go around the streamlined foot of the sail, it

smoothly breaks up the oncoming waves, and stand over the torpedo room. A 'Lockout Trunk' is there that transfers the Seals from within the submarine to the outside water environment – similar to the New London experience. From the outside, the Seals can swim to aft of midships where the Dry Dock Shelter is located (DDS). It sits on top of the deck and houses the Seal Delivery Vehicle (SDV). Another way to reach the DDS is to come up the after hatch directly into the DDS middle compartment. You'll get squared away on this system over at Coronado, "

"We'll take a quick tour below deck and show you where you will berth while underway. Let's go in through the sail . Notice the multiple antennas. There's a Global Positioning Antenna and a receiver to detect the radar from planes, ships, and surfaced subs."

"The big breakthroughs are the cameras mounted on masts that replace the old optical periscopes. Then there's antennas for receiving and transmitting high data rates for satellite communications on a super high frequency (SHF)."

This first compartment is the torpedo room. Mk 48 AD torpedoes, mines, and missiles are launched from four tubes below in the hull. They are ejected by an air turbine pump (ATP) that draws in water to the tubes. Shutter doors open when ready to launch. We'll pass through to Command and Control where all systems are integrated – sensors, countermeasures, navigation, and weapon control run by a system called AN/BYG-1. Watch the knee-knocker, that's the watertight door we'll pass through. Above us is the Lockout Trunk."

"We're in the berthing area that can house up to 119 bunks. There's a section set aside for the Chiefs that we call the 'Goat Locker'. You 'Riders' will berth in there with them. Nothing personal – all personnel not part of the ship's company are called riders. In fact, the first ship's company to be stationed after launch are called 'plankowners'. This will give some privacy and you won't be subject to so much 'scuttlebutt'."

"The next compartment houses the reactor. There are two major breakthroughs in this system. This boat is the first to use the new 50 year reactor core instead of the earlier one that had to be replaced at midlife. The other great advantage is the electric propulsion drive. It eliminates the noisy mechanical geared down drive shaft and lets the boat run much quieter. Future boats won't have these changes installed until around 2031. So we're a pilot program."

"The reactor process is nuclear fission, the splitting of uranium atoms to produce heat. Control rods in the reactor manage the process. This device is called a 'pressurized water reactor' because it is surrounded by a closed loop water path that is pumped around the reactor to absorb the heat, then flows through a steam generator to turn the water there into steam. The reactor water is kept under pressure to keep it from boiling. After transferring its energy, this water is pumped back to the reactor to be reheated. The nonradioactive steam from the steam generator spins turbines that drive the electrical generator to produce electricity for the grid and the propulsion motor. The used steam is then condensed and cooled back into water and pumped back to the steam generator to be reused."

"That's it in a nutshell. I don't mean to go on but we're mighty proud of the state of the art in this ship. I guess I won't see you guys again until we launch."

"Thanks a million Chief," Jack replies, "it was quite an education."

"I agree," Tom adds, "an amazing war machine!"

The two quite impressed Seals then returned to Norfolk to prepare for their training at Dam Neck and hopefully weekend liberty.

Virginia Beach

Tom drove the Navy vehicle to his home that was located a few blocks from the beach. It was a small rancher that Mary and the girls loved. She was a petite feisty young lady with obviously a tomboy background and she loved her man. But it was difficult to maintain a stiff upper lip during his absences. She knew what was required of him and did her best to keep a normal household for the children.

"Guess who's here girls," he said as he picked both up in his arms. They squealed and hugged him while Mary kissed him and admiringly stood by. Sarah was ten and Ava was six and thanks to Mary they were well adjusted children.

"Let's go to the beach this evening and have a cook-out," he suggested.

"Sounds good, I'll get everything ready, "Mary adds.

The beach was nearly empty so they built a bonfire

and roasted marshmallows. The girls had been swimming and the cool late afternoon air kept them close to the heat from the fire. Mary became serious for a moment and asked Tom about his assignment, knowing full well he could only give a guarded reply.

"Well, I'm not for sure, maybe a month, but I do know that we'll get underway next month after the commissioning."

"Your partner Jack, what's he like?" she tentatively asked.

"He's a professional, well decorated, and an excellent friend. I know you would like him."

"Well bring him over before you leave. Is he married?'

"Yes, his wife is in San Diego but will be here for the commissioning."

"Great! We'll have to get together."

Monday came around too fast and it was time to report to Dam Neck.

Dam Neck

"It's just about five miles south of the Naval Base Jack. We'll keep the car and commute. How about staying at our house instead of the BOQ."

"Ok thanks. Dam Neck – that's an odd name."

"Yeah, the story is that a man and a woman were walking over a bridge there and someone heard him say that he hopes she falls and breaks her dam neck. But that's an old wive's tale. Around here they call a peninsula a neck and there are a lot of beaver dams plus a dam for a grist mill was here years ago – that's more like it. Well here we are, let's check in."

"There's actually three military installations here," Tom explains, "the Naval Air Station Oceana, the NAS Oceana Dam Neck Annex, and the Joint Expedition Base Little Creek and Fort Story where I trained with Seal Team 6. But we're going to the Annex for the training."

"Here we are, Quarterdeck Building 127, Taylor Hall."

"Good morning, I'm Lieutenant Mitcher, the Junior Officer of the Day (JOOD). Let me see your orders so that I can endorse them, Chief Cody and Petty Officer Burns. Ok, let me have your pictures taken and make up your badges."

"Thank you," they both respond.

"By the way sir, we'll be commuting daily instead of staying at the CBQ," Tom adds.

"Very well, I'll issue a car pass for you."

Their training will begin in one of the buildings that come under the Navy Warfare Development Command. The Navy Continuous Training Environment Program will provide instructors from the Battle Force Tactical Engineers.

"Gentlemen, I am Lieutenant Commander Johnson and this is Petty Officer Franks. Our job will be to teach you to operate an antidrone system and also to dismantle it knowing the operational sequences – in other words make it unusable as fast as you can so you can get the hell out of there! We don't have a 'need to know' for this mission but we are aware that North

Korea sends hundreds of camera drones over the DMZ to collect data on weapon installation locations. South Korea is introducing antidrone systems to counter and obviously North Korea is doing the same, especially knowing that our Marines can employ drones to recon terrain when making landings. In fact, North Korea has saturated their airspace with SAM missile systems and early warning radar, any intrusion in their airspace will be observed. Our response is Satellite surveillance, Joint Star side looking radars from aircraft skirting around the perimeter of the country, and U2 overflights. North Korea may not be up to the state of the art but it is formidable."

"Let's get on with it. There's a company in Germany, called Aaronia, that has designed and manufactured an antidrone system that is probably the world's best. We know that North Korea has installed these systems along the DMZ and on the west coast in the region of Pyongyang. These systems have a 5km range at a 1km height but to ensure coverage, they place them close enough for the coverage areas to overlap."

"The system can be portable but these are semi-permanent. Even so, satellite coverage is reliable for locations. There are three major components; a jammer module adjacent to a console that has a map and drone location display, a frequency spectrum display showing the drone operator frequencies, and a command and data display with a keyboard. On the opposite side is a tracker antenna. The range is broadband, 9khz to 20ghz which covers nearly all the bands including radar through to satellite communications, especially S band."

"The tracking antenna that covers this large frequency band is able to detect drones in 360 degrees with direction and altitude."

"The jammer module is a high power 3D antenna array which can transmit up to several hundred watts of power. And the jammer and tracking antennas are connected to the Command Center with intelligence drone software."

"The remote control frequency analyzer has a new software plug-in to allow decision making regarding the interdiction of an intruding drone. This system can record 24/7 up to 4 Terabytes a day - amazing!"

"We'll walk through a routine:

* The system has detected a drone and its operator is at a distance of 5km. The map display shows the position and direction of the drone and operator.

* Software now gives an acoustic and visual warning, including the drone type.

* As the drone approaches the protected area, a decision can be made for countermeasures.

* The Command Center sends a signal to the jamming device telling which sector to jam.

* Once the jammer is active, the drone can't be controlled by the operator anymore – the threat is eliminated."

"Ok, now we'll walk through an actual drone intercept and let you both operate the equipment. Then we'll tear the system down over the next couple of days and show you where the vital electronic components are that need to be removed and how to erase the operating software. This will be a critical exercise to allow you to depart quickly and silently."

Newport News Shipbuilding

Tom and Jack along with Mary and the children attend the launching of the new attack submarine. The Secretary of the Navy has asked the Ambassador to the United Nations, to do the honors of Christening the boat as the USS Richmond. She swings the bottle of champagne at the bow that is draped with American Flag bunting. Everyone cheers as the bottle breaks and the black hull is slowly shuttled down the tracks from the shed to the drydock. There the drydock is closed up and water starts to flow forth from 12 pipes until 100 million gallons has lifted the ship off of the dollys and sets her afloat.

"Look Tom," Mary excitedly says, "that must be the new captain."

"You're right," Tom replies, "It's Captain George Carver, what a background. He was first in his class at the Naval Academy and quarterback of the football team that went to the Orange Bowl."

"Yes," Jack chimes in, "very distinguished, tall and rangy as a quarterback would be. He went on to get his Masters in Electrical Engineering at the Naval Post-graduate School in Monterrey. His experience comes from serving in the Los Angeles class submarines as executive officer."

Mary shyly comments, "He's a very handsome black

gentleman especially with that elegant David Niven mustache."

"Hey Mary, you would notice that," Tom chides. Jack just stands there and smiles.

"What's next," Mary asks.

"Well," Jack replies, "she'll move around to the Naval Submarine Base at Sewell's Point and join Submarine Squadron 6. Then she'll go out for sea trials."

Tom adds, "Chief Parker told me that the sea trials would only last a couple of weeks because of the strict Quality Control and Reliability programs. But they'll take the new crew and some of the consulting engineers and do a good shakedown."

"That'll work for us Tom," Jack remarks. "We'll be at Coronado next week and maybe have a week leave before we depart."

"That would be great, Jack. Is your wife coming to visit before you leave? Mary asks.

"Yes, she's practicing law in San Diego right now but will be here for the Commissioning."

"Oh, we've got to meet her and get together for a cookout at the beach," Mary adds.

"Thanks, I know you'll like her – her name is Patricia."

Naval Amphibious Base, Coronado, California

"Good morning! I am Chief Powers from SDVT-1. I represent our headquarters at San Diego. We do have attachments at Little Creek and Pearl Harbor but this assignment has top priority. The Naval Submarine

Warfare Group 3 (NSWG-3) mission is to develop expertise in deploying special warfare assets from submarines. It is interested in three things; SDV's, Dry Dock Shelters, and Advanced Seal Delivery Systems."

"You will be given an accelerated introduction to the deployment and operation of an SDV in order to serve as backup for the primary operators from SDV-2. That's their full time job but in case of an emergency, you'll be there. They are qualified as Navy Special Warfare Boat Operators (SB), formally known as Special Warfare Combatant Craft Crewmen (SWCC). While undergoing your training, a third party observer from the USN Diving and Manned Hyperbaric System Certification Authority will watch you train to make sure that the operating procedures are correct and that you are in compliance. He is a Certification Technician and a Master Diver, which I am also, so I'll be in the water with you and your team. Naval Intelligence wants this mission to be letter perfect. We'll meet tomorrow at 0900. A mockup of the Dry Dock Shelter and SDV are in the tank. We'll do a dry run without water to familiarize you with the apparatus. Tomorrow afternoon, Navy Transport will ferry us up to Bremerton, Washington. That location and Puerto Rico are two places where water visibility is good for training. You will meet your team there. A Seahawk helicopter will take all six of us out to the USS Dallas and drop us off. After the training period, we'll embark onto the sub and return. Have a good evening."

SDV and Dry Dock Shelter
Public Domain - US Navy Photo

The Tank

"Let's talk about launching the SDV from the Dry Dock Shelter. We open the front hatch door on the flooded rear hanger compartment of the shelter and swing it all the way on its hinges until it clears the open pathway for the SDV that's shaped like a torpedo. A man is then stationed on each side of the SDV with a tether line attached to the vehicle while two more men stand by each side or rear. One cranks out the track then all pull together and bring the SDV out onto its track clear of the shelter."

"The operator pilots then pull back the canopy and climb aboard. One will be the pilot and the other a navigator. The combat team then joins them in the rear. While the pilot activates the electric propulsion, the navigator enables the navigation and camera consoles."

"This Mark 8 Mod 1 SDV is built of fiber glass reinforced plastic non-ferrous material to leave no magnetic footprint. Since the propulsion system consisting of battery, electric motor, and controller, all have magnetic fields that can be detected by mines, active shields are employed using currents to cancel the magnetic field strength – by about 21 db."

"The 'free flooding' environment requires the Seals to be under water in their scuba gear which enhances their readiness for the mission. There is a Doppler Inertial Navigation System (DINS), a submarine Rendezvous and Docking System (RDS), and a side and forward avoidance sonar – Obstacle Avoidance Sonar (OAS). A little on the navigation system, it continually calculates position, orientation, and velocity from a known starting point received from GPS – the initial orientation. It's very accurate."

"The propulsion is an electric motor with a five blade propeller driven by a rechargeable silver-zinc battery that has a storage capacity of 148 kilowatthours minimum. She can go to 150 feet at 9 knots using 521 kg of ballast. Demolition items can include MK 4, MK 5, and MK 36 limpet mines that can be attached to a hull. Limpet stands for sea snails that cling. "

"She carries compressed air to extend the range of the swimmer's tank. The maximum noise level allowed is 80 dbA, like a passing car, which I personally think is too high."

"Climb inside and check the instrument panel that is waterproof. First, there are two masts, navigation and communication, that can be raised from lying flat on top of the SDV to a vertical position and extended above the surface."

"A display of the sea surface is located between two horizontal rows of pink pushbutton switches for operation by the navigator. The pilot side shows the heading, depth, and longitude and latitude. A similar arrangement of pink pushbutton switches are above and below that display with a standalone compass mounted nearby. An operating stick controls the rudder and trimtabs. Let's check our gear and be ready to leave after lunch."

"Right chief," Jack replies, "see you at the hanger."

Bremerton, Washington

"We'll meet the team over at the Naval Base Annex and wait for the helicopter pilot to file his flight plan and do his preflight check. You know Naval Base Kitsap is the third largest in the nation behind Norfolk and San Diego." Chief Powers announces.

"This is my first visit here," Tom replies.

"Yeah, me too." Jack adds.

"Well, here we are. Let me introduce our SB specialists Petty Officers Rusty Draper and Jerome Black, meet Jack and Tom."

"It's a pleasure guys," Rusty says enthusiastically. Jerome concurs.

"Here comes our Certification Observer," Chief Powers notices, "Meet Chief Purdue."

The Chief replies, "I'll be hovering close by but not to be in your way. Take your time and if we need to repeat, that's ok."

"It's time to head for the hanger," Chief Powers orders.

The big MH 60 S Seahawk was warming up with its blades turning as the six men approached.

"When we get aboard you'll have time to get on your gear." Chief Powers shouts.

The pilot and copilot begin checking the instrument panel while the men are climbing aboard. This helo has the ability to be loaded for bear with Hellfire missiles and machine guns someone noticed.

"Get comfortable men," the pilot announces, "we have large sliding doors on each side of the cabin. I suggest three of you disembark on each side so you'll all depart together. We'll hover about ten feet above water for a short drop."

She lifted off easily and headed toward the rendezvous with the submarine. "We'll travel about 155 to160 mph, that's 135 to 140 knots, it's 102 miles from here to the Pacific and then another thirty miles to the sub. So we'll be cruising for about an hour."

"Let me brief you while we're underway," Chief Powers suggests. "The water temperature here will be between 48 and 54 degrees. Fortunately, it's sunny so we should have good visibility below. As you know, we'll be using the full face mask with the underwater transceiver. It's good down to 200 feet. Good quality sound but a little tinny like an old speaker. These things operate around 25 to 33 kilohertz. When we arrive, the pilot will contact the sub which will be at periscope depth."

As they traveled along, conversations took place on mundane things just to kill time. Jack said that he remembered an early scheme for underwater communications. "They called it 'frequency shift keying'. The voice messages were digitized into 1's and 0's. Then a frequency F1 represented the 1's and a frequency F2 represented the 0's. The frequencies were transmitted through the water and converted back."

Tom adds, "Yeah, the latest studies are called LIFI for subs, laser light flashes 0's and 1's. It's like a Morse code but blinking so fast that the human eye couldn't see them. The question is how well do photons travel through water. NATO has created Janus for underwater communication guidelines – they're really into this subject. The visible light spectrum is so much greater than the Radio Frequency spectrum – plenty of room for more channels without disturbing the RF."

The pilot interrupts, "We're approaching our destination. Put on your scuba gear."

"USS Dallas, this is Skyhawk. We are on station and ask permission to begin exercise. Over."

"Skyhawk , this is USS Dallas. Permission granted. We are ready to bring on the team through our Lockout Trunk when training is complete. Over."

"Thank you USS Dallas, the team is ready to start."

"All right men, carry on and good luck."

All six men jumped from the helo down to the water surface and entered smoothly as the Skyhawk turned

Seals Unloading SDV From Shelter
Public Domain - US Navy Photo

and headed east.

"Boy, that cold water just hit my neck – cold," Tom thought as he braced.

Tom and Jack swam to the front door of the Dry Dock Shelter through the slightly opaque water. The observer took a treading position about ten feet away with Chief Powers. The SB experts took up positions alongside the shelter to wait for the door to open. Jack opened the door of the flooded compartment and pulled it around to clear the track. One of the SB Seals cranked the track out from the shelter with the manually operated winch. Tom and Jack then grabbed the tether lines and started to pull the SDV out of the shelter. The SB men came along side and helped to push the vehicle. Jack and Tom could feel the strain on their quads while trying to swim and tug the vehicle free. "A little more Tom," Jack said through his transceiver. It was a hands free device that communicates in cycles, transmits for thirty seconds, receives for twenty seconds, transmits for thirty seconds in that order.

The SDV was clear of the shelter. Jack and Tom pulled back the canopy doors on each side while the SB Seals steadied the vehicle. Jack climbed into the navigator seat while Rusty Draper joined him as pilot. Everyone climbed in at this point since the sub was going to move. Rusty energized the system and motor while Jack set the navigation controls and raised the antennas for a GPS fix. He then communicated with the sub to announce that they were ready. The sub responded that they would begin to slowly cruise at 4 knots. Rusty said to go astern of the boat and prepare to circle around the sail while it was underway.

Jack thought, "Here we go!" They made a wide swing around the stern and came back up on the other side with bubbles leaving a trail behind the SDV. They crossed in front of the moving sub and headed aft again. "Change places Jack, take the helm." They circumvented the sail once again after almost losing sight of the ship from behind. This time it was a fairly close call while crossing the sail with an audible beep from the sonar avoidance system. On other occasions, SDV crews took hours to find their host.

Tom and Jerome repeated the process successfully as Tom said to Jerome, "This is an eerie feeling, cruising around that large sail while it's heading right for us at four knots."

Jerome laughs, "Give her a wide berth, she's coming

hard by!"

Tom lets out a huge laugh which catches everyone's attention. The Certification Chief then said that he felt comfortable with the exercise and Chief Powers agreed.

"All right," Chief Powers said, "Jack and Tom take control and bring the SDV back to the shelter with the Rendezvous and Docking System."

They maneuvered the SDV at 9 knots until it was over the track leading to the shelter, then slowed down to 4 knots and hovered over the moving sub. They contacted the sub and said that they were ready to land. The sub came to a stop, Tom turned the bow down until they made contact. The SB Seals exited and grabbed the tether lines. The SDV was secured, Jack and Tom exited with the Chiefs and closed the canopy after shutting down the systems. They shut the Shelter door and looked things over.

The sun was low on the horizon which started to darken the waters. Eight hours had elapsed without realizing it. The men swam over to the forward Lockout Trunk and entered the water filled area. The hatch was closed and water evacuated. Air filled the trunk and the men exited to the interior of the submarine where they met the OOD who congratulated them for a good exercise. The sub rose to the surface and headed back to the base. It was 11 pm when they arrived so Chief Powers and Purdue bid the Seals farewell. Tom and Jack headed to the commissary for a quick meal and beer with Rusty and Jerome. The training would be documented and forwarded to the Executive Officer of

Seals Operating SDV
Public Domain - US Navy Photo

the USS Richmond.

"You know guys," Jack muses, "there's got to be a better way to get the SDV out of the shelter. Why can't they design a motorized drive to crank the track out of the shelter, then have a driven pulley system pull the SDV out of the shelter onto the track – that would save a lot of time. The Seals could unhook the tethers and be on their way."

"Great idea, Jack," Jerome submits, "put a suggestion into one of the SYSCOM's divisions . You might have a patent there with a little more detail."

Rusty chimes in, "The Naval Facilities Engineering Command (NAVFAC) is a good one. They're close to you at the Washington Navy Yard."

"Thanks, I think I will, and thanks for all your help so far. I'm sure our mission will be a success."

"Amen to that!" Tom adds.

Virginia Beach

"Jack, I think we need to do some running and work-outs to keep in condition. Also, I'd like to get to the firing range and practice.

"Good idea, I'm with you," Jack replies, "we've got the rest of the week."

"When's your wife coming for the commissioning?" Tom adds.

"Today! I can't wait to bring her over here to meet you guys."

"Great, we'll have dinner at my house," Mary said, "so be sure and bring her here."

That evening it was clear and cool, perfect for a stroll on the beach. Mary was waiting as Jack brought in Patricia. She was tall, elegant, and soft spoken but Mary sensed a reserved shyness or an underlying tension.

"Welcome Patricia, I do hope we can spend some time together before the men depart."

"Yes, I look forward to it and call me Pat."

Later Mary served a full course dinner after which they all took an extended walk along the shoreline as the small waves washed across the sand.

"Pat, how about coming over tomorrow morning while the men are off doing their thing?"

"Ok, be glad to, it'll be good to get away from those close quarters at the base."

The next few days were well spent together, that

rare occasion when two people with similar interests come together and bond. Finally, one morning, Pat seemed to be especially anxious and confided to Mary. "How do you keep going like this every time a mission approaches?"

"I try to keep the household normal and pray a lot knowing that Tom will do the best he can regardless of the situation."

"Well I've had to go through this for sixteen years and I can't take it anymore. My nerves are so bad I can't concentrate on my legal work at the firm. I even take tranquilizers to get through the day. Yet we still have four more years of this before he retires. I have to decide, do I continue this way or do I leave him?"

"Oh Pat, don't do that! He told Tom that he wants to study to be a minister in the Church of Christ back in Muskogee after he retires. His faith is everything. And you, with that singing voice of yours would fit perfectly in the a cappella style of music that the Church prefers."

"I know, I just don't think I can hold up."

"Well, take care of yourself and let your faith guide you."

Sewell Point

It was time for the commissioning of the USS Richmond, SSN 802. Jack and Tom were invited to stand with the crew for the ceremony. The crew was lined up across the deck in their dress whites on both sides of

Commissioning of a Navy Submarine
Public Domain Image

the sail. Two gangways ran across from the pier to the deck with bunting and the letters USS Richmond. Captain Carver was officially offered command of the USS Richmond by the Commodore of Submarine Squadron 6. He accepted the command and gave a short speech where he challenged the crew to be the best for God and Country.

Afterwards, Mary had plans to celebrate the departure of the men with Pat at a fashionable restaurant in Norfolk. They were scheduled to get underway tomorrow evening. However, Pat was absent.

Jack had appeared to be in anguish while he stood at attention on the deck during the ceremony. And now, he explained why - Pat had left and gone home! She said that she was going to leave San Diego and go home to Muskogee where she would find work with a local small law firm. She couldn't take it anymore. Whether or not she would stay with Jack was to be determined, yet the mission had to go on. He had to buck up, bite the bullet and focus on his responsibility hoping that she would not do anything.

The next day saw the crew busily preparing to get underway. Jack and Tom had brought their gear and weapons on board and were getting assigned to their quarters. Shortly after, the announcement came to station the underway watch.

Mooring lines were lifted and the sleek vessel slowly made its way from the landing while the OOD and lookouts stood their station on the sail. It would slowly maneuver into Hampton Roads, head Northeast over the Hampton Roads Bridge - Tunnel, then due East to the Chesapeake Bay Bridge - Tunnel.

Mary knew that the Richmond would be going over the Chesapeake Bay Bridge-Tunnel soon, so she and the children drove the three and a half miles to Island number 1 on the bridge in spite of the fact that the Chesapeake Grill Restaurant there had been permanently closed. They stood on the east pier and waited for the submarine and her husband to come by.

The sun was setting with a brilliant display of color that put a red tinge on the darkened small clouds. Soon the USS Richmond slowly made its way over the bridge tunnel. The submerged front of the boat created white wakes on each side of the bow that complemented a reflected red glow on the sail. Mary watched as the majestic war machine rounded Cape Henry and headed into the dark eastern sky and open sea.

CHAPTER TWO

"All Ahead Full"

The USS Richmond maintained a steady course and speed of 10 knots until the second day out when she received a radio message about upcoming weather off of the Cape Hatteras coast. This area has historically been noted for dangerous weather conditions dating back to first recorded history and the numerous shipwrecks attest to that.

"Conn, radio, incoming Priority Traffic, Weather reports a northeaster storm with 60 foot waves will arrive within the next ten hours at 35.248 degrees Latitude and 75.539 degrees Longitude."

"Radio, conn, acknowledged."

"That's Cape Hatteras Commander Slater," Captain Carver notices. "Set course for Norfolk Canyon where there's deep water."

"Aye sir," replies the OOD.

"Helm, conn, left standard rudder. Set course one two ze-ro."

"Conn, helm, steady at course one two ze-ro."

"Helm, conn, maintain 10 knots."

"Conn, helm, maintain 10 knots, aye."

"We'll get there in 6 hours and beat the storm," the Captain says.

"Yes, it's about 50 miles from our position," the OOD replies.

Back in the Chief's quarters, Jack and Tom are checking their gear. "You know Jack, riding in a sub is like riding in an airplane, smooth and without turbulence except for a slight vibration of the engines. You hardly realize that you're moving."

"Yeah, but I'm curious about one of those deep dives, probably feels like a roller coaster. By the way, one thing wasn't covered thoroughly in our SDV exercise. There are three compartments in that DDS shelter."

"From what I've heard," Tom replies, "the forward most compartment is the hyperbaric chamber for treatment of the injured divers. The middle compartment, also called the Transfer Trunk, is where entrance and exit from the sub takes place, of course the third is the hanger for the SDV. We'll probably use the Transfer Trunk instead of the Lockout Trunk since we're on board."

"Well, we better get back to checking our gear while we have the time," Jack suggests. "Ok, let's lay out everything on our bunks."

Brain bucket helmet
Night vision goggles
Body armor
Weapon suppressors to reduce gas and flash
Heckler and Kock HK416 rifle with lasers
Sig P226 handgun
M79 grenade launcher
Sights
Grenades

Fixed blade
Bolt cutter
Breaching charges
Magazines for vest
Flashlight
GPS watch
Gloves
Small piece of detonation cord to wrap around door knobs
Camera
Chem lights, infrared
Gerber- pliers, wire cutters, strippers
Two tourniquets
Celox wound dressing
Water

"Check, Jack"

"Check! We won't need the grenades or grenade launcher Tom, even the camera."

"Yeah, and I hope we won't need the Celox. Oh, I forgot to include my Tomahawk."

"What?" Jack exclaims.

**Tomahawk
Public Domain**

"Some of the Seals are using them now. Good for breaching, getting in doors, small locks, and of course hand to hand combat."

"Where do you guys get them?"

"A fellow in North Carolina, name's Daniel Winkler, first made them for the movie 'Last of the Mohicans' and got recognition. He's modified them somewhat to fit our needs. They're called 'primeval tomahawks', officially WK11 Stealth Ax."

"That's really cool Tom, you gonna wear war paint with that?"

"Ha, not a bad idea!"

Later that evening the OOD reports to the Captain that they have reached Norfolk Canyon.

"Conn, helm, steady at 34.345 degrees Latitude and -71.427 degrees Longitude."

"Helm, conn, steady as you go."

"Mr. Slater take her down to 200 feet."

"Yes sir, Captain."

"Dive, conn, make your depth two ze-ro ze-ro feet. Announce as you go."

"Conn, dive, descend to two ze-ro ze-ro feet. Announce in 10 foot intervals, aye."

"Mr. Slater," the Captain adds, "two hundred feet is more than adequate. Two thirds of the wave energy is under water meaning that the 60 foot wave is one third of the total height so two thirds of the total height is a 120 foot disturbance under water. We'll be below all the ebbs and currents of the rough seas."

"Yes sir, point taken."

"Notice that Tom, we're starting to descend. Not too steep, it seems. Now I know why the ondeck crew has seat belts, they can go down at a twenty degree angle."

"Probably more, according to the COB Chief."

"Tom, while we're alone I've got to say that I can't get my situation off of my mind. I don't want to lose Pat."

"Of course you won't. It's obvious that she really cares for you. And she knows that the rest of your tour will be spent recruiting and teaching."

"Well, keep us in your prayers."

"I already have!"

"Here comes the COB, Chief Parker. He's always good for a laugh," Tom adds while trying to get Jack in to a better frame of mind.

"Gentlemen," the Chief announces, "I see you're about your business. Do you have everything you need?"

"Thanks Chief," Jack replies, "we think so, we'll know for sure when we get briefed from Pearl."

"Tom, I just noticed your tomahawk, that's something else," the Chief adds.

"Yeah, it started as a motivator with Seal Team 6 but it has become a useful tool," Tom explains.

"This moves me," Chief Parker admits, "I want to do something. My great grandfather gave me a feather charm when I was a child that Chief Quanah Parker had given him. I've kept it with me all these years while on duty. It symbolizes honor and connects the holder with his Creator. You're going into combat so I want you to have it. Connect it to your tomahawk. It's an eagle feather with a hook for fastening. It will be good medicine!"

"Thank you Chief, I'll try to honor you and your people while on my mission and hopefully the good medicine will let me bring it back to you."

"I'm off duty, let's go down to the auto-dog and have a few laughs, come on."

"Sounds good Chief, I hope the ice cream in that auto-dog has some good flavors." Jack adds.

Chief Parker was noted for his standards regarding the crew. He was boss but he was fair along with being strong and firm. He didn't mind getting his hands dirty when working with them nor chewing them out when needed. But there was another side that heightened the respect that the men had for him. He could tell jokes, do impersonations, and keep people in tears with laughter. This was one of those times when he would entertain in his pajamas and slippers, adding an eccentricity to his character.

"Tell us some stories Chief," Tom urges.

"Ok, I read this one by Dr. Jerry Bread. Creeks and Cherokees had a war in the late 1800's. No one was winning so the Cherokees decided they would use dynamite. They bought some dynamite and started throwing it at the Creeks. But the Creeks won because they lit the fuses and threw them back."

Jack and Tom roar with laughter. A few off duty sailors gathered around and this encouraged the Chief to do more.

"A redneck told us to go back where we came from, so we pitched our tent in his backyard."

"Hey Chief, how come you're so smart," someone shouted.

"I don't know, back in first grade I was the only one to count up to three and get two of the numbers wrong."

The whole crowd laughed until the tears flowed and he laughed with them.

"But seriously," he added, "my prayer is quite simple, 'O Great Spirit, I seek strength not to be greater than my brother but to fight my greatest enemy – myself'."

"Here, here," Jack replied and they all raised their glasses in salute.

Back at the chief quarters, Chief Parker gets inquisitive, What does it take to be a Seal candidate?"

"Before anything," Jack replies, "you have to pass a Seal Physical Screening Test – you've got to be in darn good shape."

"There's some minimum requirements," Tom adds, "a 500 yard breaststroke or side stroke, 42 pushups, 50 situps, 6 pullups, and a one and half mile run in 11 minutes."

"After that," Jack continues, "a more rigorous physical training at Warfare Prep School for 8 weeks, then BUDS for 24 weeks. Each man is then assigned a specialty that he is suited for, and trains to become expert in that discipline, continuously with thousands of hours input."

"What are your specialties," the Chief asks out of concern for their skills for this mission.

"I'm in to Surreptitious Entry, Electric or Mechanical," Jack explains, "I carry lock lube, shims to open padlocks, lock picks – rakes and tension wrenches to move tumblers , also a cold soldering iron."

"I selected Advanced Close Quarter Combat," Tom adds, "room by room clearing of an intact building with enemy combatants and noncombatants. Firing stances, weapon positions, and reflexive shooting with minimal collateral damage."

"Sounds like you're the men for the job," the Chief respectfully adds.

"How do you keep training, stay in shape, and then go into harm's way all the time?"

"It's very simple," Jack replies, "God has our back".

Tom nods in agreement and says, "If you don't have Faith, forget it."

Panama Canal Zone

"Helm, conn. Set course for one nine ze-ro."
"Conn, helm. Course set for one nine ze-ro."
"Helm, conn. Maintain ten knots speed."
"Conn, helm. Maintain ten knots speed, aye."

"Captain, this will set us at 9 degrees 28 minutes North and 79 degrees 55 minutes West, the entrance to Limon Bay and Cristobal. I estimate three days run time since we're just about in the vicinity of GTMO."

"Very well. We'll anchor in Limon Bay. It's a good shelter from the sea and close to Colon where our Operator is located. He'll pilot us through the Gatun Locks, past Gatun Lake, and through the Miraflores Locks in about eight to nine hours."

"It'll be interesting Captain, to see the Canal again and the changes. The expansion to accommodate the huge container vessels went from 100 feet wide to 180 feet wide and the length went from 1000 feet to 1400 feet. The ships are raised 85 feet above sea level in those locks."

"Yes, I'm glad the upgrade was made. The Chinese have been speculating on a large canal in Nicaragua but they had some problem with the local government about the ecology of the waterways. Anyway, we're scheduled to pick up our Operator in the evening upon our arrival for a night run through."

"No liberty this time Sir!"

"Afraid not."

Pacific Ocean

"Commander, set the Port side watch for getting underway."

"Yes sir, and shall I give the Canal Operator your regards, his boat is coming along side."

"Please do, he did an excellent job."

"Lookouts aloft, inform me when the boat is away."

"Conn, lookouts, boat has cast off and is away."

"Helm, conn, Set course one six ze-ro and speed at ten knots."

"Conn, helm, set course one six ze-ro and speed at ten knots, aye"

"Lieutenant, after we pass Taboga Island set course to one eight ze-ro. Once we're off of Combutal Peak, set course for two nine ze-ro to Pearl, Latitude 21 degrees 19 minutes North and Longitude 157 degrees 50 minutes West."

"Mr. Slater, we have 5200 miles to cross, at ten knots it will take 21 days. Plan to submerge and set speed at 20 knots, we have a schedule to keep. While in route we'll perform maneuvers, especially the deployment of our towed array. I want to see if there is a problem with the baffle area in the water behind that might affect our sonar tonal reception."

"Very well Sir, I'll alert Sonar."

Chief's Quarters

"Tom, when we get to Pearl, let's ask permission to take our weapons to the firing range while the ship is being loaded with fresh fruits, vegetables, and other supplies . It'll also take some time for the skipper to get our operating orders from Naval Special Warfare Command (NSWC) and COMPACFLT."

"Good, I want to get more time on the HK 416. They're not a whole lot of difference from the old M-4 model but the front sight's been changed to a folding design and it has a new pistol grip."

"Right Tom, it's still a honey with a firing rate of 700 to 900 rounds a minute and the Stanag magazine holds thirty rounds. We could use the 100 round Beta C – Mag drum but we're going to be in and out quick. You ever fire it under water."

"No, and I hope I won't have to! By the way, I should have mentioned it before, instead of the Sig P226, I brought a Glock 19, you can't destroy it and the frame is light plastic. It holds 17 rounds and the trigger pull is half that of a revolver at 6 pounds. The Safe action trigger uses a striker instead of a hammer. Also takes a silencer. It's been approved by NSWC for Seal use."

"Ok, sounds good, I'll get one at Pearl. Chief Parker says that we'll be in route for about eleven days. We can start working out in the torpedo room, more room there. They squeezed in a treadmill, rowing machine, and some dumbbells. We can hang a bar across the doorway for pullups."

"All right Jack, I'll also run in place, do pushups, squat with weights, and lots of crunches. When can we get in to use the area?"

"The crew works out after coming off watch. We can work around that unless there's a drill."

Captain's Stateroom

"Come in Commander, have a cup of Joe."

"Thanks, Lieutenant Stuart is acting OOD while I take a break."

"How's the crew shaping up in your view?" the Captain inquires.

"Very well, very professional, especially Lieutenant

Stuart. Outstanding performer – she was in the top ten percent of her class at Annapolis."

"Well, I'm afraid we'll still have to comply somewhat with the operational pause set up by Admiral Richardson, Chief of Naval Operations. He's directed Admiral Phil Davidson, US Fleet Forces Command, to manage the investigation into operational tempo, personnel trends, material, maintenance, and training, all on a tight timeline."

"I can see why," the Executive Officer replies, "after the USS McCain and USS Fitzgerald collisions at Singapore and Japan occurred, there was a shakeup in command. Vice Admiral Phil Sawyer is now commander of the 7th Fleet."

"Yes, the Navy has been complaining that the pace is unsustainable – unrelenting operational demands with a limited supply of ships. Senator McCain asked Admiral Richardson if it was true that some sailors have 100 hour workweeks. Admiral Richardson said that he wouldn't deny that."

"I think sir, that the Budget Control Act and sequestration have had a lot to do with it."

"I agree, and the nuclear sub fleet has had its share of collisions over the years, so we're going to have to keep the crew motivated to do their best, maybe even win the coveted E. And, I'm sure we're going to hear more about this at Pearl."

Pearl Harbor Naval Base

"Mr. Slater, make arrangements to have the classified AID drone brought on board and integrated with the launch system at one of the torpedo tubes."

"Yes sir. Shall I arrange with Security to screen the area of all non-engaged personnel?"

"By all means. Keep me posted on the progress, especially the launch system interface."

"Aye sir. I'll cover all of the technical details"

"In the meantime, I will contact PACFLT and get an appointment to meet with them at the Nimitz-MacArthur Pacific Command Center headquarters. It's about five miles from here at Camp H. M. Smith. We'll have to coordinate the Naval Special Warfare Command (NSWC) chief with the COMPACFLT commander, both have to be present."

Headquarters

"Gentlemen, my name is Captain Winslow, adjutant, and I will brief you on the mission statement by means of a Power Point presentation. The specific details will be in the operational orders for the assigned personnel two days after the USS Richmond has left Pearl Harbor."

"The CIA has confirmed Operation Mongoose with the President after ascertaining that the conditions for success, based on the North Korean political posture and the satellite imagery of the prevailing geographic conditions, will give a probability of success at ninety percent. As far as official policy is concerned, North

Korea and the United States rely on the intelligence community (IC) of their countries. North Korea however, has to depend on open source intelligence (OSINT) such as news media, social media, and publicly-available information which includes American television. Whereas, the United States has satellite coverage of every activity in North Korea."

"The John Hopkins University School of International Studies has a group called 38North for the exclusive and continuous analysis of North Korea's politics and economic status. They have used commercial satellite imagery to discover missile sites, submarine development, plutonium processing, and even agriculture yields."

"North Korea's position based on 38North input, is that the United States President's military saber rattling carries no weight. Only if all administrative officials come together with one policy will the rogue regime take notice. The Secretaries of State and Defense want diplomatic solutions and now the President calls for the same but while brandishing a big stick."

"If North Korea had geospatial intelligence it could decide from US military movements whether action is forthcoming. Our former Director of National Intelligence said that North Korea would never give up nuclear weapons which to them says that the United States has accepted this view."

"So where does that leave us? It becomes necessary to remove the leadership of the country in order to have the replacement power be inclined to negotiate."

"The present dictator is ruthless. He feels that a

strong nuclear arsenal will hold the United States at bay. In six months he will have a hydrogen bomb and intercontinental missile capability. He wants things to stay as they are and not escalate into war. To solidify his hold on power, he has executed 340 people, 140 of which were senior officers in government, military, and the Korea Workers Party. He has eliminated his powerful uncle and half brother. His ultimate goal is to have a treaty with the United States and its allies to remove the US presence from the Korean peninsula. China feels the same way."

"We have studied the dictator's daily routines and habits. He does frequent inspections of military bases and state run factories around the country. Because of the desire of a traitorous faction of the military to overthrow him, he uses multiple vehicles for hiding his presence. He tours the East coast on his Princess 95MY yacht with some of his more trusted generals. To demand a high level work ethic among the citizens, he has a 6 am wakeup call for the city of Pyongyang through the use of loud speaker music, just as he does around the clock at the DMZ. He does enjoy horseback riding but indulges the sport only with security measures."

"After all of the scrutiny made to find his vulnerability, it has been in vain. Because of the constrained life style, his paranoia about the loyalty of his military, innuendo from friends and associates about subversion, the safety of his family, and finally the knowledge about Plan Jupiter where the CIA and the South Korea Intelligence Service tried to send terrorists to use biological and chemical substances against his supreme headquarters, he has abdicated!!"

"He has fled to Switzerland where he was educated and fortified a villa for himself and family. The grounds have a private airfield, armored vehicles, a company of secret service personnel, along with loyal household servants, chauffeurs and pilots. His favorite yacht is anchored in the harbor of China's Yulin Naval Base on Hainan Island in the South China Sea. Billions of won currency have been placed in Swiss banks with investments in the Bahamas and Bermuda."

"Where does that leave the country? A cabal of power hungry and pugnacious members of the officer corps are trying to overthrow each other by taking control of various parts of the military under the guise of reunifying the administration. The missile sites and nuclear bombs are up for grabs to be sold to the highest bidder, be it Iran or Syria. There is only one solution, we must act quickly to eliminate these people by way of the plan that is on standby."

"Basically, we have the USS Richmond armed with an intelligent attack drone that will be satellite guided to the target, moving or stationary. Navy Seals will clear a path through the antidrone systems for the AID drone to have clear access to the target. It will be a stealth mission that will occur under the North Korean radar screens. Once the mission is complete, South Korean officials will contact North Korean civil servants from cities and towns along with military officers to offer help in redefining the government by providing a constitution and elections."

"We have a window of opportunity here. North Korean antidrone systems are limited to defeating the command communication to the enemy drone whereas the United States Navy has a 30 kilowatt 'Athena' (Advanced Tesla High Energy Asset) laser system that will strike a large armed drone and heat it until it burns. Sooner or later, North Korea will have these state of the art systems. Just in case, the AID drone has a coat of shiny aluminum that will reflect 85 percent of the laser beam. Only one sixth of the energy would be absorbed."

"Gentlemen, I will start the particulars by pulling up the Yellow Sea map. Captain Carver and Commander Slater, you will provide the specific operational details for the Seals after your departure from Pearl."

"The Yellow Sea, which by the way does have a yellow tint from the sand dust blowing off of the Gobi desert, is not deep which makes it difficult for the submarine to navigate but which also appears to the Koreans as being not a viable place for attack - our advantage."

"Your boat, Captain, will have to remain considerably off shore in 200 feet of water. Any closer and you'll be in 65 feet of water. So the SDV will have about a 2 hour run or 20 miles to shore. I recommend that you replace the silicon-zinc batteries with lithium-ion. They'll give longer life. Too bad the advanced SDV long range design was cancelled."

"The average depth for the Yellow Sea is 144 feet with 260 feet in certain areas. But the numbers I gave you were in the vicinity of the landing zone."

"Look at the Pyongyang area on the display. Just

slightly to the Northwest is the coastal landing zone. Go due North of Chungsun until you hit the coast. That'll be the Seal landing location. The coordinates are 39.2438 Latitude and 125.3798 Longitude. This location is 31.6 miles from Pyongyang. It's a rough hilly area with wide coastal plains. There are dozens of small islands around and the sea has large tidal swings, sometimes seven feet high but two feet on the average."

"About the target. On October 10, a public holiday is held to celebrate Party Foundation Day – the founding of the Central Organizing Committee of the Communist Party back in 1945. There will be public speeches and a military parade in the large square of Kumsusan Palace of the Sun. This is where Kim ll-sung and Kim Jung – il, the father and grandfather, are entombed. All of the Generals will be gathered on the bandstand to watch the fireworks at night followed by the Korean's People Army parade. The timing will be determined by satellite and communicated to you. Your Seal attack on the antidrone sites will require precision timing. The target coordinates are Latitude 39.0268 and Longitude 125.7826.

"The Palace is located in the Northeast section of Pyongyang at the intersection of the Hapjang and Taedong Rivers. The drone is to take out the target with zero damage to the Palace."

"Back to your entry by way of the Yellow Sea. It is recommended that initially you cruise using the 'sprint and drift' approach in order to monitor the sonar tonals. There could be antisub mines, Cluster Bay mines for shallow water, and Cluster Gulf mines in deep water. As you proceed North through the Yellow Sea to Korea Bay, in the middle of the sea is the Huk-san Mud Belt, made from clay and silt. The Yellow Sea warm currents and the Korean Coastal Current cause this fine grain sediment. The Belt extends about one third of the width of the sea. When you deploy your towed array, be careful that it does not lower at slow speeds and drag the bottom."

"Finally, The Korean defense is formidable. They have a 146,000 man coastal navy with 130 hovercraft. It's a brown water navy with 780 vessels including 70 Yuno and Sang-o midget submarines. Most important are their 20 Romeo submarines with proximity torpe-does and their Kilo class destroyer with two helicop-ters. The best weapons are their 43 guided missile pa-trol boats with SS-N-2ASTYX antiship missiles with radar and infrared homing systems. Of course this defense applies to both East and West coasts. Naval bases are scattered around the West coast so be alert for shore patrols. That about does it. One more thing, Admiral Richardson's operational pause will be placed on hold in your case, the mission can't be interrupted. You will proceed to Guam and load your torpedoes and missiles there. Good luck and God speed!"

USS Richmond

"Hey Tom, look who's here. Hi guys, when did you arrive?"

"We just flew in from Bremerton," Rusty replies,

"had to hold some last minute training sessions."

"Yeah," Jerome adds, "we thought that we were going to miss the assignment, but the brass said to shake a leg and get out there. This must be top priority."

"Well, we'll find out soon enough when we leave here," Jack adds.

Tom then jumps in and says, tongue in cheek, "We got a nice sendoff from the Admiral over at Naval Special Warfare Command. He said that we had been picked for our outstanding experience, commendations, and special training – that was quite an honor! Maybe I'll make Chief after this."

"Yeah, and maybe the only easy day was yesterday!" they all shouted back in unison, while laughing.

Pearl Harbor Submarine Base

"Here comes the Captain with two Marine guards", one of the deck hands says quietly.

"And he's carrying a locked briefcase handcuffed to his wrist," another adds.

The guards then salute and depart as he goes aboard. A short while later he reappears on the sail with his executive officer.

"Take her out, Mr. Slater," the Captain orders.

"Aye Captain, line handlers, single up all lines," as he shouts over the bullhorn. The order was repeated by the sail phone talker over the sound powered telephone to the phone talkers on deck. They replied that all lines were singled (every line was removed except for a single line at each station).

"Cast off all lines," the OOD orders.

"All lines cast off," the phone talkers reply.

"Helm, conn, slow ahead,"

"Conn, helm, slow ahead, aye."

"Helm, conn, left full rudder."

"Conn, helm, left full rudder, aye."

"Helm, conn, meet her."

"Conn, helm, meet her, aye."

"Helm, conn, steady as you go."

"Conn, helm, steady as you go, aye."

"Helm, conn, left standard rudder."

"Conn, helm, left standard rudder, aye."

"Helm, conn meet her."

"Conn, helm, meet her, aye."

"Helm conn, ahead one third,"

"Conn, helm, ahead one third, aye."

"Helm, conn, steady as you go."

"Conn, helm, steady as you go, aye."

"We've cleared the entrance sir," the OOD remarks.

"Very well, set course 2 6 ze-ro for Guam, Latitude 13.3622, Longitude 144.5141."

"Yes sir, helm, conn, set course 2 6 ze-ro."

"Conn, helm, set course 2 6 ze-ro, aye."

"Helm, conn, set standard speed ahead."

"Conn, helm, set standard speed aye."

"Mr. Slater, did you notice the Arizona as we pulled out?"

"Yes, sir, the Missouri battleship was also impressive."

Chief Parker, COB, addresses some of the crew in the mess area. "Listen up men, I want to talk to you while you're here for lunch. We'll be crossing the International Date Line in a few hours and everyone will get a diploma."

"A diploma Chief?" one of the seamen asks.

"Yeah, you graduate into tomorrow and your certificate will give you a membership into the 'Domain of the Golden Dragon'."

"Oh come on Chief," someone shouts.

"No, seriously, the Date Line is an imaginary vertical line that separates the Eastern Hemisphere from the Western Hemisphere. It lies between Alaska and Siberia and runs from the North Pole to the South Pole with some zigzag around Hawaii and Samoa. If you go from West to East, subtract a day, if you go East to West, as we're doing, add a day. So set your watches ahead a day. By the way, our ship's time is synchronized with Greenwich Mean Time in London like all submarines. Any questions?"

"Ok, let's turn to."

Captain's Stateroom

The four Seals along with the COB are seated at the conference table when Captain Culver and Commander Slater walk into the room. "Don't rise gentlemen, stay seated," the Captain suggests while waving his hands in a downward fashion. "Mr. Slater, you may place your key into the safe lock and I'll do the same thing with mine. We'll open together."

The safe is opened and the skipper takes out the envelope marked "TOP SECRET".

The Captain begins, "The purpose of this meeting is to review the classified operational plan for the Seals. It will be very specific to leave no detail unturned. The operative word in this mission is timing. We will procced into the Yellow Sea and cruise North until we enter Korea Bay. Thirty miles East from the western coast of North Korea is Pyongyang, where our target the Kunsusan Palace of the Sun is located. Due to the shallow depth of water, the closest we can get to shore is twenty miles. You all will take the SDV and reach land in about 2 hours at the rate of 9 knots."

"Prior to your departure, you will be briefed on the location of submerged mines that our AN/BLQ-11, Long Term Mine Reconnaissance UUV will map."

"Your job will be to create a free access zone through the antidrone network for the AID to reach its target. Once launched, the attack drone will travel 51.6 miles in about 31 minutes to the target. Their antidrone units have a range of 5 kilometers. All of the units are spaced 8 kilometers apart to allow overlap of 2 kilometers of the coverage to prevent gaps in the search. The entire coast is arranged this way."

"From your point of arrival on the beach, it will take you 4.5 minutes to run the 1 kilometer or .62 miles in full gear to the first unit. You have the coordinates.

Five minutes will be allowed to take out the men and the system. But what is VITAL is that you do not take out the first unit until immediately after they call in their hourly all clear. This will buy you an hour before the alarm goes off. So set your watch to Korean time.

"Next, you will cover the next 8 kilometers or 4.97 miles in 36.5 minutes at the same rate. Take out the second unit in 5 minutes which raises the elapsed time from the call-in to 46.5 minutes. Heading back to the SDV in 4.5 minutes raises the total time from the call-in to 51 minutes – plenty of time left to overcome any obstacles and board the SDV and disappear, assuming all goes well. After the next 9 minutes, the alarm will sound and helicopters will come to search."

"The second VITAL instruction is that as soon as unit two is down, you communicate to the military satellite from your GPS unit the stored message in Comanche language 'we have a Geronimo.' The satellite will convey the message to the submerged Richmond via the A2RF expendable buoy which has RF to Acoustic gateway at the water's surface and the attack drone will launch."

"Weather wise, this time of year is pleasant but windy. The typhoon season just ended but there are strong currents. The current flows from North to South at a rate of 1 meter per second so keep that in mind, you may have to make corrections in your SDV heading from time to time. The Hydrographic Office in Washington has sent us wave direction and height along with the current velocity."

"Another thing, Algae grows in abundance, especially across on the Chinese side. You can walk on the beach there and never see sand – all green. People can lay in it and cover themselves, it's not poison but it consumes large amounts of oxygen which harms marine life. North Korea has recognized its value as a fertilizer, superfood, and oil source. To try and counter the imposed sanctions, they are creating ponds and farming the stuff though with minimal effect on the economy. So be careful at night, there are 258 acres being worked."

"I understand you may know some basic words in Korean, Jack."

"Yes Sir - hello, I'm lost, things like that that may be useful for entry."

"What about the drone. Why did we create a special design for this mission? The Navy did consider the Reaper MQ-9 but it was too big. Then they considered the Predator MQ-1B but it was too noisy with that 4 cylinder motor."

"The Defense Advance Research Project Agency (DARPA) has combined the best features of two experimental drone programs, the Blackwing drone and the Sea Robin drone,"

The Blackwing is designed to operate in an anti-access and aerial denial environment, It has the ability to talk to submarines, carry an electro-optical and infrared payload (EO/IR) that extracts the target from background clutter through use of the IR sensors and algorithms, it utilizes an anti-spoofing module (SASSM) that synchronizes drone instruments with satellites for communications, of course GPS, and a secure Digital Data Link (DDL) that connects one location to another for the transmission and reception of digital information. "

"On the other hand, the Sea Robin XFC can also be launched from a submerged submarine with similar operating systems. Our AID drone will unfold like the Sea Robin into an X wing format. It will be powered by an electric motor instead of the piston motor using a Hydrogen Fuel Cell as a source. The Hydrogen combines with Oxygen to make electricity with water vapor as the exhaust. No telltale residue. This will be a real stealth drone with low acoustic and thermal signatures."

"The warhead will contain PBX-9, a highly explosive anti-personnel munition that's been around since

Sea Robin XFC
Public Domain - US Navy Photo

World War Two. Unaffected by small arms fire, it has one and a half times the energy of TNT. It will self-destruct upon command if the mission is aborted."

"Since the drone will cruise at fifty feet, it will use a sophisticated terrain following system similar to Lidar's sensing technology that illuminates the ground with an invisible laser beam and then analyzes the reflected data for integration into the autopilot system."

"Finally, the communication system for tracking the target. The CIA will initially inform a Gulfstream G550 aircraft of the itinerary of the target. The G550 carries the Joint Stars side look radar which has a wide area surveillance capability to permit tracking of vehicles and people. Because of the extreme coverage by the North Korean air defense systems, the G550 follows the territorial borders with the ability to reach an altitude of 51,000 feet."

"Next, the encrypted target data is transmitted to the military satellite that covers the area in sync with the earth's orbit. This spy satellite has a 2foot resolution – it could see a ball being tossed from 90 nautical miles. The satellite then goes into a track mode with the target and informs the submerged submarine via the SS SSIX Spherical Intelligence Submarine Satellite Exchange System by way of the A2RF buoy. Target coordinates are then loaded into the AID drone computer. The drone computer sets the initial flight data while still in the launch cannister. Launch occurs from the torpedo tube, the cannister detaches, electric propulsion starts and the drone then monitors real time satellite data to update the flight plan. All target movement is tracked by the satellite and delivered to the mobile drone. Once on station, and after the satellite informs us of the status, I will make the decision to attack unless informed by PACFLT to abort. If it's a go, the drone homing command sets in, the missile is armed, and pursuit takes place."

"It may be considered redundant, but once the satellite is sending encrypted navigation/guidance commands to the drone, the Joint Stars radar tracks the drone and the target and sends feedback to the satellite for correction which would be minimal yet confirmational."

"That's it gentlemen, our next stop is Guam to load the missiles and torpedoes."

Chief's Quarters

"Say, Chief, why doesn't the Air Force just bomb the country and take out the airfields, naval bases, and military encampments?" Tom asks quizzically.

It's very simple," Chief Parker replies, "the airspace over North Korea is one of the world's most dangerous. Their defenses cover most of the country. Stationary and mobile radar units provide information for their SAM missile sites. If we would fly below the radar nets, numerous antiaircraft guns, manually operated, would be immune to cyber and electronic warfare. Low flying craft would also be exposed to thousands of shoulder-fired surface to air missiles."

"That brings up a good point," Jack adds, "is the

drone susceptible to their shoulder fired missiles?"

"It's not impossible but very unlikely," the Chief replies, "the drone is flying at night about 100 miles an hour, fifty feet above the ground. By the time it passes a given point, the enemy wouldn't have time to respond. And of course, the drone is completely silent with the electric motor."

"Well, that's comforting," Jack acknowledges.

"Jerome, you're an ET, electronics technician," Tom questions, "how are the transmissions encrypted to avoid interpretation?"

"One way is to vary the carrier operating frequency to prevent detection. They usually do that at what they call an FM rate, so the drone receiver has a wide frequency band for reception. Another way is to change the transmitted data. Information is in binary code, zeros and ones, if you have a string of these and change some of the zeros into ones and some of the ones into zeros, then the message is garbled. But it would have to be done systematically with for example an arithmetic series. It's an equation with a bunch of terms starting with a value in the first term, then the second term is the value plus a constant value, the third then is the value plus 2 constant values, and so on. On the receiving end, the same equation applies from the same starting point to see which bits were reversed."

"Enough already!" Tom shouts, "Holy smokes, leave it to the engineers."

"Ok, sorry, Jerome laughs, "I get carried away."

Later when Tom and Jack are alone, Jack says, "We've both had a lot of missions and have been lucky.

Do you ever have survivor's guilt?"

"Well, some of my shipmates have rested their oars but no, thank God," Tom replies, "I know some other guys that have taken to booze or have had breakdowns but I'm doing ok. The biggest lesson to learn is mental toughness. Be alert, never get comfortable, put others before yourself and get down on your knees and admit that God has a plan, not you – and be thankful for that."

"Well-said Tom," Jack beams, "you sure you're not a candidate for the ministry?"

"Ha, no, I'll leave that to you!

Naval Base Guam

The USS Richmond has rafted up to the submarine tender USS Frank Cable AS-40 (along side) in Apra Harbor to load munitions.

"Captain, one of our retractable tie down cleats is locked in place. We can't roll it for the lines," says one of the Officers on deck.

"I'll have Mr. Slater send Lt. Stuart over to Camp Covington with a requisition for the Seabees to make the repair immediately."

"Thank you sir," the Officer responds.

Later the Captain announces over the 1MC shipboard announcing system, "This is the Captain. All meals for the crew will be served on the tender while we load. Our officers will dine with the Captain and officers of the tender this evening."

That evening while dining on board the Frank Cable, Captain Culver asked about the background of their namesake. The sub tender captain was quite taken and began to speak, "Frank Cable was the Naval Architect that piloted the first submarine in the US Navy – the USS Holland SS-1 in 1897. She carried 3 torpedoes with one tube and had an 8 inch deck gun that propelled the projectile with compressed air – the explosives in that day were so unstable,"

"Your sister ship," Captain Culver adds, "the USS Emory S. Land AS-39, is she stationed here?"

"Yes, but we have to cover the Western Pacific, so one of us is always here while the other covers the area. Admiral Land, by the way, founded the Merchant Marine Academy at Kings Point. He was also involved in submarine design during the 20's and thirties and was head of the construction of 4,000 Liberty and Victory ships during World War Two."

"That's quite a record," Captain Culver replies, "your ships couldn't have been better named."

The time- consuming job of loading munitions would continue around the clock. At first, twelve Tomahawk missiles were placed in the two six- gun shooter launch tubes. These UGM-109 missiles are designated for land attack and carry 1,000 pounds of explosives. Next, 16 of the MK48 AD torpedoes, the best in the world, were loaded one at a time in the holding area. Following this, 4 Harpoon UGM-84 anti-ship missiles were also loaded with the torpedoes but wrapped in buoyant capsules to fit into the torpedo launch tubes.

Last but not least, eight of the latest design of the

ADC M4 Acoustic Device Countermeasures decoy were placed in the submarine signal ejector rack in the event of an enemy torpedo attack.

The ship to shore telephone then rings while the crew is preparing to shove off. The JOOD answers and receives a priority message.

"Captain Culver, you're wanted immediately over at the captain's quarters on the subtender."

"Did they say why?" he replies, "We're getting ready to get underway."

"No sir, but it sounded urgent."

The Captain, Mr. Slater, and Chief Parker enter the room where the serious captain and his executive officer are seated.

"I'm afraid that I have some troubling news Captain, the depth estimate and the distance to shore in the Korea Bay are incorrect. The Hydrographic Office sent us a TOP SECRET priority message regarding the correct status of the Korea Bay. In order for the Richmond to be submerged in at least 157 feet of water, she's got to be 64 miles away from the landing zone. The SDV doesn't have the range."

"How in the hell did Hydrographic screw up like that," the Captain burst out, "we were told it was 200 feet and twenty miles from the landing zone."

Everyone suddenly became subdued, the Captain had never lost his composure before now.

"The Korea Bay is constantly changing with the continuous runoff and fast currents. Buoys and beacons are constantly being changed around, Corrective data is continually coming in," the captain volunteers as an attempt for atonement.

"Do we have to abort the mission?" Captain Culver cautiously asks.

"Hopefully not, but time is of the essence. The new Dry Combat Submersible S302 has been Mil approved. She's thirty-one feet long, 7.7 feet high, and is fully enclosed with 24 hours of stored air. The Dry Dock Shelter DDS will have to be extended 9 feet to accommodate her. We can have Lockheed Martin in Palm Beach Florida get one here overnight. The Seabees will work around the clock to extend the DDS. In the meantime, we'll remove the SDV. When the DCS arrives, the SB specialists can enter the DCS and become familiar with the instruments while the Seabees are working. The operating technology is about the same as the SDV. She has the range but of course 64 miles will take time to traverse."

The new submersible did arrive and by way of Lockheed Martin's C-5M Super Galaxy transport. Tom and Jack were relieved to not have to be in scuba gear for a long period.

"Mr. Slater, let's get underway."

"Very well Captain," the OOD replies.

"Now hear this, Starboard watch take stations for getting underway."

"Conn, underway watch manned and ready."

"Single bow, stern and spring lines," the OOD announces over the bullhorn.

"Conn, bow, stern, and spring lines singled," the JOOD replies.

"Cast off spring lines," the OOD orders.

"Spring lines cast off," the JOOD replies.

"Set SPM, Secondary Propulsion Motor 90 degrees to Port," the OOD orders.

"SPM set to Port," the JOOD replies.

The stern then starts to swing to Starboard away from the tender while the Bow moves slightly forward in toward the tender. The handlers let out slack on the stern line as she moves.

"Stop the SPM, set SPM to zero degrees," the OOD shouts as the ship's stern continues to swing slowly out.

"Line handlers, cast off bow and stern lines."

"Conn, bow and stern lines cast off."

"Helm, conn, set speed to one third astern."

"Conn, helm, speed one third astern."

"Helm, conn, right standard rudder, slow speed ahead."

"Conn, helm, right standard rudder, slow speed ahead, aye."

"Helm, conn, meet her."

"Conn, helm, meet her, aye."

She heads North out of Arpra Harbor until Point Polaris is reached off of the Starboard bow.

"Helm, conn, left full rudder."

"Conn, helm, left full rudder, aye."

"Helm, conn meet her."

"Conn, helm, meet her, aye."

"Helm, conn, steady as you go."

"Conn, helm, steady as you go, aye."

The Richmond then proceeds slowly west until she passes the end of the island at Point Udall.

"Captain, did you notice the THAAD missile sites as we pulled out?"

"Yes, it gives me a feeling of confidence."

"Helm, conn, set standard speed."

"Conn, helm, standard speed set."

After sailing out into the Pacific Ocean for two hours, the Captain orders the OOD to set course for Latitude 33.6409 North and Longitude 124.9365 West.

"Helm, conn, set course 315"

"Conn, helm, course 315 set."

"Mr. Slater, take her down to 400 feet Altitude (depth). Shift reactor's main coolant pumps into fast speed, then proceed to flank speed. I want to operate at 100% reactor power for a few hours to test the system. After two hours, reduce speed to standard speed, place coolant pumps in normal mode. Then, place sonar in passive mode and maintain conditions until we reach the Yellow Sea."

The Captain exudes confidence but in the back of his mind he is concerned about the 8 hour wait needed for the Seals to return while the enemy is reacting to the attack.

CHAPTER THREE

"Take Her Down"

"Captain, we've reached the entrance to the Yellow Sea. Jeju Island is off of our starboard quarter. The South Korean Coast is four hours away."

"Good, Mr. Slater. Reduce speed to three knots and come to periscope depth after dark. I want to feather out the antenna so the water won't leave a wake behind it."

"We will deploy the TB-23 towed sonar array at that time. I don't want to spend time turning right or left at intervals to clear baffles even though our cavitation is low." (Baffles is the area in the water behind the ship which blocks sonar reception due to cavitation and the wake. Ships have to turn sharply to observe the blind spot. The towed array would extend far behind.)

"Yes sir, understood."

Two Days Later

"Not much activity Captain, a few fishing boats. Aside from the patrol boats and submarines, we need to be on the lookout for the China National Petroleum oil rig. It's presently supposed to be 120 kilometers (75miles) west of Nampo, Pyongyang's port."

"Yes, near our area of operation. The problem is that the rig is a jack-up oil rig – it's movable. They use it to drill test wells, in fact they've drilled about 16 in this area already. Could be a problem if a lot of boating is there, wherever the latest well will be. All right, let's get to our station. Set course for Latitude 39.1544 and Longitude 124.4586. There better be 157 feet of water there. Set depth at 100 feet."

"Aye Captain. Helm, conn, set course bearing ze-ro ze-ro five."

"Conn, helm, course set for bearing ze-ro
ze-ro five."

"Dive, conn, set altitude to 100 feet."

" Conn, dive, altitude set to 100 feet."

"Helm, conn, set speed to 2/3 standard."

"Conn, helm, speed set to 2/3 standard."

"Mr. Slater have the towed array cable deployed in 'short stay' (shortened). We can still get audibles in these shallow waters, I don't want to have it drag."

"Very well, sir."

"The only way we're going to hide here is to find a thermal layer to lie under, if we're lucky. Launch the SSXBT bathythermograph and collect data for temperature versus depth."

"Yes sir, at once."

The three-inch diameter SSXBT is then launched from the signal ejector and rises to the surface. The float separates from the lifting body and continues to ascend. At the surface, the probe and the intermediate spool for the tether wire deploy and the float immediately scuttles. The probe then starts to transmit temperature until it reaches bottom where the tether is cut allowing the components to scuttle. The onboard recorders and processors use Windows to output the data for use by the BSY-1 computer to determine sonar and fire control solutions.

Thermal layers or thermoclines occur when temperature changes abruptly for fairly small changes in depth. This causes water density to change resulting in the layers that act as barriers to sonar energy. Sonar transmission from ships is reflected and scattered, so while below the layers, submarine's sonar performs poorly.

"Captain, I don't think we'll have much luck in this shallow water. My guess is that we'll have an isothermal situation – constant temperature through the entire depth."

"I agree, if the temperature data is unchanging, cancel the order."

"Yes, sir."

October 9 - On Station

"Mr. Slater, maintain 100 foot altitude, all stop, and call all the Seals to my stateroom."

"Very well sir, shall I call Chief Parker to attend."

"Oh yes, definitely."

"Good morning gentlemen, the steward is on his way with coffee, have a seat."

"Good morning sir," they all respond in unison.

"We're on station at last. As you've been briefed, we are 64 miles from your landing zone. That'll be about an 8 hour run in the new submersible. Prepare to get underway at 0800 tomorrow. That'll put you near shore about 1600. The water depth there is 19.6 feet, so your vehicle can remain secure. Temperature in this area during October averages 53 degrees with a high of 66 and an overnight low of 42 degrees. There's a minimal chance of rain with sunshine 72 percent of the time. There are 11 hours of daylight with dusk at 1830. A reminder, the current flows North to South this time of year with a rate of one meter per second."

"Most important are the submerged mines. We launched the AN/BLQ-11 Long Term Mine Reconnaissance UUV to collect this information and return. It has a range of 100 miles so the entire area has been covered."

After unfolding the map, Captain Culver shows the location of Cluster Bay mines and their depths. "Load this information into your submersible's side and forward avoidance sonar system (OAS) Petty Officer. It looks like about one every fifty feet for this location."

"Let's set a tentative schedule. You will arrive on location around 1600 if you can maintain 8 knots. At 1815 raise the antenna and advance the DCS closer to shore. The Richmond's floating wire UHF/VLF antenna will forward the command for you to execute the mission. Be prepared to exit and hit the beach at 1830. Get to the first antidrone unit by1845. It'll be dark by 1900. At 1904, commence your attack. Then follow your plan. The drone will now have to travel 95.6 miles, about 1 hour, with ETA at 2100. Any questions?"

"No sir,' Jack replies, "we've taken notes."

"There is a request sir, if we may ask."

"Yes, by all means," the Captain replies.

"Tom and I have prepared codicils for our wills. If you and Mr. Slater would witness them, we'll appreciate it."

"Yes we will, and we'll keep them in the safe.

October 10 – D Day

"Are the Seals on Standby Chief, ready to go?" the Captain inquires.

"Yes sir."

"I'm coming down to see them off."

Jack, Tom, Rusty, and Jerome were dressed in their XCEL Drylock Hooded Full Wetsuits, insulated for warmth with a quick dry outer lining. They wore Bates 8 inch Durashocks waterproof Boots that were a favorite of the Seals. Their tote bag had Mechanix finger free gloves, facial grey camouflage cream, extra socks and underwear, and a Chase Tactical Stricker ACH Level IIIA Combat Helmet. The weapons and operational equipment for Jack and Tom were attached to a back pack.

They stood there under the after hatch that led upward to the middle section of the Drydock Shelter. All three areas of the shelter were completely airtight.

"Gentlemen, you are about to embark on an historic mission. Stay safe, and may God go with you." He then shook hands with each one of them and looked at his watch. It was 0800.

The men climbed up through the hatch opening, walked into the submersible section, and entered the DCS.

There was plenty of room, enough for six people. Tom and Jack stowed their gear while the SB Seals started to check the operating systems. The Navigation System was programmed for the landing coordinates, the Avoidance Sonar had all of the mine locations in memory, and the air system displayed the capacity for 24 hours. Rusty tapped on the hull as a signal to flood the area.

Once flooded, the members of the submarine crew that had exited through the forward Lockout Trunk opened the flooded shelter hatch and manned the tether lines. Rusty engaged the electric motor and the 28,000 pound DCS began to back out of the shelter while being guided by the crew with the tether lines. The lines were then disconnected as the vessel turned around and headed toward North Korea.

The ride was smooth as they maintained a depth of fifty feet. Except for the quiet hum of the electric motor driving the propeller, the only other sound was the soft voices of the crew.

"We're maintaining 8 knots Jerome, with an occasional course adjustment due to the strong current," Rusty acknowledges.

"Yes, and I'm keeping my eye on the submerged mine field plot. It'll be several hours before we reach that point though."

In the back, Jack suggests to Tom that they exchange letters for their wives, just in case.

"That's a good idea Jack, if one of us doesn't come

out of this, the other can forward the letter."

"Well, I've got to let my wife know how much I care for her and the fact that after this mission I'll be up for recruiting duty but if I didn't make it I did want her to know that I hoped I could share my life with her as a minister."

Virginia Beach

Mary Burns was driving into the shopping district when she passed the Church of the Holy Family. She felt an urge to pull over and make a visit. The Shrine to St. Jude, patron of hopeless cases, caught her attention. She lit a candle and prayed for the safety of her husband.

On board the DCS, Tom had a strange sensation of calm and peace. He takes it as a good omen. The hours pass quickly and then Jerome announces that they are entering the mine field, As a distraction, Tom begins to share the news of the Argentine submarine loss.

"From what I read, the snorkel that took in air on that boat while submerged quit working." BEEP-BEEP.

"It's ok guys, we're 25 feet away from them," Jerome calmly persists.

"Well anyway, the automatic valve that opens and closes," BEEP-BEEP, pause, "the snorkel had its battery shorted. She took on water," BEEP-BEEP, pause, "and went down. Then at that depth she imploded."

"It's amazing how one small incident," BEEP-BEEP, pause, "can cause havoc," Jack adds.

The strained conversation continued until one more beep- beep. Jerome then announced , "Ok guys, we're all clear. We'll be at our landing point in about twenty minutes. Then we'll settle down until we go ashore."

It was 1630 when they reached this destination, one half hour later than predicted – not bad.

"In an hour from now, we'll need to gear up and be ready," Jack suggests.

"Ok, one final check on equipment," Tom adds.

At 1815, the DCS is moved closer to shore in ten feet of water. The antenna is raised to receive the VLF signal from the floating wire antenna on the Richmond.

"It'll be dusk at 1830," Rusty reminds them.

They wait anxiously for the signal to go at 1830. Then a one word message arrives a minute later – "Quanah!"

Jack – "We're on!"

Tom - "Let's roll!"

Tom then put on his backpack and goggles, went to the lock-out hatch located amidships of the DCS and entered. He placed the temporary oxygen mask on while the trunk filled with sea water. The hatch then opened, he took a deep breath, removed the mask, and swam through the murky water until he felt bottom about fifty feet away. Carefully standing up, he removed the goggles and mounted the combat helmet with the 4 Tube Night Vision Goggles (GPNVG-18) which gave him 97 degrees of vision instead of the forty degrees on the older twin models. The NVG amplified the low- level light and displayed a green phosphor screen which was best for differentiating shades of objects.

Jack was soon beside him and they glanced around

for their target. Jack noticed it, pointed two fingers to his eyes, then pointed one finger ahead. Tom nodded and they waded through the rest of the water with the glistening black wet suits, protruding four eyed goggles, and H and K rifles at the ready - looking like some harbingers from the lower regions.

They begin to jog in the twilight toward the enclosure that houses the antidrone system. Some Algae plots are seen and carefully bypassed to avoid slowing their progress. Tom reminds himself to maintain pace over the .62 mile in order to be there by 1845. He notices the effect of the severe drought on the potato and soybean crops while passing the stunted growth. Then he recalls that he is probably running through human excrement that is being used as fertilizer per Kim Jung Un's orders. It was highlighted on the news that a deserted North Korean soldier had numerous parasites in the stomach due to the bad practice. Jack points to a distant greenhouse that is another attempt to overcome the food shortage.

It appears that the site is operational, two North Korean soldiers are inside, one overlooking the controls, and the other lounging on the daybed. Jack points to his watch, it is 1900 and dark. The building is dark inside except for the instrument panel red lighting. They hear the men talking and assume that they are getting ready to make their hourly contact to control command. A phone call, then the receiver slams down.

It is 1904! Jack wraps a piece of detonation cord around the locked door knob with 2 turns and a slip knot. It is filled with PETN and will explode with a primer. He sets it off, the explosion opens the door slightly then Tom kicks it the rest of the way. The startled North Koreans turn and reach for their weapons. Jack fires first with his laser guided beam and suppressor mounted rifle. He hits the soldier in the chest, the man goes down while Tom hits his man in the chest and follows with a head shot. The first man is still moving so Jack places another round into the man's temple. It is over.

Jack places the system into a shutdown mode to avoid any abnormal transmissions due to a fault in the operating sequence while being dismantled. Tom takes his Tomahawk and damages the tracking and jamming antennas while Jack pulls the mother board from the harddrive and puts it into his backpack. They leave. It is 1910 – they are one minute behind schedule!

They check their compass and set the direction for the next location. The five mile run is expected to take 36.5 minutes so they push a little bit more to make up for the lost minute. The ground is hard except for an occasional sandy area. They try to avoid the rugged hills scattered around and the garden plots while constantly scanning left and right with their green magnified images. It is 1945 as the second site is approached, allowing for the 4 minute delay at the first location to make sure that the check-in call was made.

The door is open! Jack calls in Korean - ahn-nyong (hello), jam-shi-man-yo (excuse me / just a minute). One of the two soldiers moves to the doorway while the other stands behind him. When they see the Seals, Tom fires and hits the first one between the eyes. He falls out of the doorway while the other one tries to duck down. Jack fires and hits him in the upper leg. He tries to move back inside. Tom finishes him with another shot. They enter the building and begin to damage and dismantle the system as before. Just as Jack grabs and packs the mother board while Tom is damaging the antennas, a shot rings out and then a second – Jack goes down. Tom's reflexes act quickly, he slings the Tomahawk over in the direction of the firing source and hits the combatant in the face with the blunt end of the spinning weapon which cuts through his ear. The man screams and Tom shoots him in the middle of the chest followed by a head shot.

He looks down at Jack and sees that half of his face is gone – jaw, teeth, chin, and part of the nose. He grabs the Celox Hemostatic Agent and pours it on the face, then applies pressure for thirty seconds. It combines with the blood to make a gel plug. He then covers the injury with Celox Hemostatic gauze and gives Jack a shot of Morphine. Realizing that two rounds had been fired, he looks around to see if the second one had hit. It did, blood was flowing from the hip area. He cuts open the wet suit and applies Celox Rapid to stop the arterial bleeding. With minimal compression the bleeding was halted. The Celox Chitosan granules will hold the dressing in place fifty times stronger than regular bandages.

Jack began to groan, then slowly stopped as the Morphine took effect. He began to whisper, "Pat, help me." Tom started to lift Jack but he gurgled something that made Tom lean down closer to his face.

"Leave me, you can make it, I can't."

"You can't? Like hell you can't!" Tom shouts.

"You know dam well when you think you're done, you're only 40% done! We're outa here."

Tom then drags Jack over to the doorway, steps outside and sends the GPS signal to the satellite. He repeats and the satellite responds with an affirmative, "We have a Geronimo." He struggles through the doorway with his comrade and lifts him and the backpack onto his back with a fireman's carry as Jack groans and becomes silent. Tom kicks his elbow back into Jack's side, he hears a grunt that acknowledges that his friend is still alive. He then straightens up, adjusts Jack for ease of carry, and starts toward the DCS which is still six tenths of a mile away. He mumbles to himself, "It's a good thing I've been doing a lot of power lifting, this guy's heavy."

The USS Richmond had been hovering on station at periscope depth with torpedo tube one ready and the outer door open. When the signal for a clear drone track arrived, the order to launch was given.

"Torpedo room, Fire Control, shoot tube one."

"Fire Control, Torpedo Room, shoot tube one, aye."

The Torpedo Air Turbine Pump (ATP) pulled in sea water, then drove home the piston that ejected the drone and canister. It shot to the surface tethered by a fiber optic cable. At the surface, the canister shell separated from the missile and sank to the bottom. The fiber optic cable with preflight instructions disengaged after the wings unfolded into the X wing formation and satellite commands were being recognized and received. The drone oriented itself into the proper low-level attitude and proceeded on its mission.

Captain Culver then ordered the Richmond to settle near the bottom to gain maximum depth. Realizing that their weapon would cause extreme defensive measures, he ordered the ship to rig for depth charge, maintain the shortened towed array and the sonar in passive mode for maximum coverage, and the Helm to standby for setting flank speed operation.

"Mr. Slater, reload tube 1 with Mk 48 AD torpedo."

"Aye, aye, sir."

It was now 2010. Tom had covered a third of the distance to shore after the destroyed antidrone stations had missed making their hourly check-in call. This situation resulted in an immediate response by two North Korean land- based Z-9 Harbin ASW helicop-

Z-9 Harbin Helicopter
Public Domain Image

ters equipped with two Mk 46 style lightweight ET-52 anti-submarine torpedoes and French HS-12 dipping sonar. The HS-12 very low transmitting frequencies of 3 to 5 khz allows the immersed sonobuoy to overcome non-detection areas and be omni-directional in an active or passive mode. This system nicknamed FLASH, has long range detection ability.

Another five minutes of struggle left Tom with a quarter of a mile to go to reach the shoreline. He began to faintly hear the throbbing put-put of helicopter engine noise and knew exactly what to expect. He stopped and turned to see the helos flooding the surrounding hills and flatlands with probing searchlights while heading toward the destroyed stations.

There was no way that he could cover the last leg of his escape path without being seen. Out of desperation he hurried over to the nearest Algae patch and laid Jack down against it.

"Try not to move Jack, I'm going to cover you with Algae – we've got company."

He quickly covered Jack and left a small opening for him to breathe. Then he laid down and covered himself. It was 2020. The loud helos soon arrived directly overhead with blinding light covering the area. He felt sure that they would be discovered as the helos hovered. Tension mounted when he thought of Jack possibly having a kneejerk reaction to the lights and noise. He was relieved when the searchers reached the shore and turned around to head to the shelters. The helicopters landed to investigate the loss of contact from the operators. It was now 2030.

Back on the DCS, Jerome and Rusty became concerned that Tom and Jack might be in trouble. They were way overdue so Rusty said that he would go ashore and look for them. He left the submersible and waded ashore with his HK rifle. Immediately he noticed the helo lights as they were landing and saw the silhouette of Tom carrying Jack toward him.

"Jack's hit. You've got to raise the DCS so we can get him inside. He couldn't handle an oxygen mask."

"Ok, I'll call Jerome."

He clicked on his acoustic transceiver and contacted Jerome via the risen antenna. After explaining the situation, the DCS soon showed its front end as the bow nosed onto the land. The rear of the vessel remained in water for the propeller to back them off. The hatch was exposed so Rusty carefully lifted Jack's legs while Tom shifted out from under and held his upper body. Jack started to groan as they placed him in the airfilled trunk.

They both paused from entering and looked up as they heard a soft wisp of air like a sudden breeze. It was precisely 2041 – and the AID drone was passing overhead, racing toward Pyongyang.

Tom entered next followed by Rusty. The hatch was sealed and Jack was spread out over a couple of seats. Jerome told Rusty to get in back to get some of the load off of the bow – ineffective but comforting. The DCS slowly slid back and became free of the shore. It turned around and headed toward the rendezvous with the USS Richmond.

CHAPTER FOUR

"Rig for Silent Running"

Jerome navigated the submersible along the bottom until they reached sixty feet of water. He then raised the vessel to ten feet below the surface, close enough to place the antenna upright for communication with the Richmond.

They were all concerned about how well Jack would be able to cope with his injuries over the long 8 hour run. Tom said that he would minister another morphine injection if necessary. Yet he watched for slow breathing and checked the pulse rate occasionally for a sign of slow heartbeat. He realized that morphine was an opioid analgesic with possible side effects and addiction. His main concern though was Jack's facial injury that might impede his ability to breathe.

Having seen the professional devastation applied to the antidrone stations, the helicopter pilots realized that it was definitely foreign intervention, not a local insurrection. One pilot returned to his base to report on the findings while the other started to search the sea for possible surface or submerged craft.

Captain Culver realized that within a half hour helicopters would be searching the area after damage was discovered. He felt vulnerable if he stayed on station yet he had to wait for the Seals.

It was now 2100, fifteen minutes after the submersible had left the area. A cryptic message was received on the Richmond's floating antenna from the satellite by way of the SS SSIX Satellite Exchange System. Two words – Target Deleted! The AID drone had been placed into the homing mode of operation and completely destroyed the grandstand. Bodies were scattered everywhere. The Parade had broken up as the soldiers and participants fled for cover. Ambulances arrived to find only two survivors of the officer corps upper echelon. The Paramedics administered first aid and then placed them in the vehicle for transportation to the local military hospital. They mysteriously died on the way. Confusion and panic affected the junior officers around the bases – they want orders – who do we attack – do we use nuclear?

The Z-9 Harbin helicopter was flying a back and forth pattern over the part of the sea that faced the two antidrone stations. It was searching for submarine activity with a Magnetic Anomaly Detection system (MAD). Although it had passed over the DCS near shore, there was no indication of its presence due to the non-ferrous fiber glass reinforced plastic hull.

As the helo continued seaward it finally passed the Richmond's position and received a positive response of an anomaly. A metallic substance will disturb the magnetic lines of force of the earth. The submarine's magnetic field distorts the natural field flux density by weakening its natural state and this change can be monitored. To confirm this anomaly, the helo circles around and repeats the findings to establish the location.

The towed array sonar operator detects the presence of the helicopter.

"Conn, sonar, helicopter presence observed by the high turbine RPM. It is stationary."

"Sonar, conn, very well, acknowledged," as the BSY-1 computer confirms the tonals.

"Captain, we've been detected," the OOD announces, "they must be using a MAD system."

"Then we've got to leave quickly before they attack," the Captain replies.

"Yes, Sir!"

"Helm, conn, proceed at Flank speed."

"Conn, helm, proceed at Flank speed, aye."

The Richmond propels forward at 40 knots (36 mph) as the helo drops a sonobuoy into the water for expediency rather than utilize the tethered HS-12 dipping sonar. It detects the bearing and speed of the submarine and relays it to the helicopter. The sonobuoy then floats until the seawater soluble plug dissolves and lets this sensing detector sink.

The helo reacts quickly and releases two ET-52 acoustic homing torpedoes – one from each side of the fuselage. They are a cheaper version of the Chinese YU-7 torpedo with some of the American MK46 features that had been learned by reverse engineering the purchased weapon.

As the torpedoes are released from the Z-9 Harbin, small parachutes are deployed to allow the torpedoes to drop down into the water nose first. They have a speed of 30 knots with a 6km (3.7 m) range. They sense the submarine presence and lock-on to their prey. The

Richmond is slightly ahead and will outrun them until they run out of gas and fall to the bottom. But Captain Culver is taking no chances since the AN/WLY-1 countermeasures system recommends acoustic interception.

"Fire control, conn, release two noisemakers."

"Conn, fire control, release two noisemakers, aye."

The two Acoustic Device Countermeasure (ADC) MK 2 decoys are fired from the mini launch tubes located on the bottom of the hull. The ET-52 acoustic torpedoes then start to track the closer and louder decoys that follow a course away from the submarine.

"Conn, sonar, torpedoes changed course."

"Sonar, conn, very well, continue forward monitor with the large aperture sonar array (LAB) until you receive a strong fixed return from the Chinese National Petroleum Oil rig."

"Conn, sonar, continue forward monitor, aye."

"Helm, conn, reduce speed to 2/3 standard."

"Conn, helm, reduce speed to 2/3 standard, aye."

The USS Richmond quickly covers the 36 mile distance to the oil rig through a bearing determined by the sonar tonals that had identified it. The submarine then assumes a hovering position on the north side of the rig in order to avoid exposure to active sonars on enemy ships that may be approaching the original coordinates. Captain Culver knows that enemy vessels will be alerted at the Nampo and Haeju bases to interdict any planned escape route. He is also aware that the submersible will not return to station for 7 hours so he will wait and then try to make contact. His concern is well founded, who will arrive at the station first – the enemy or the Seals?

Four hours has elapsed and the submersible is approximately halfway to the rendezvous point, while the Seals are unaware of the transpired action.

"Jerome, Rusty," Tom quietly says, "Jack is struggling with his breathing."

"Is it the morphine?" Rusty asks.

"No, the body fluids in the injured area are choking him. I keep trying to swab out his throat but I'm probably causing trauma. I'm going to have to perform a tracheotomy."

"The medical kit is mounted on the rear bulkhead," Jerome rerplies, "it has every contingency covered."

"Good, Rusty, can you come back and hold his arms so he wont jerk away?"

"Yes, we're on a steady course, no problem."

"I'll give him another morphine injection. We'll wait a few minutes until it takes effect. Raise his shoulders, put something under them for elevation so that his head will bow down some to expose the neck."

"Good, now hold his arms down from behind his head. I'm going to get ready to start."

Tom pours alcohol on his hands and unwraps the scalpel. He makes an incision in the anterior region of the neck – about an inch long. Then he makes another incision in the trachea (windpipe).

"This hole will do the job but I want to play it safe. There are three parts to the insertion of the breathing tube. Keep holding."

He inserts the outer cannula (curved tube) with the thin obturator tube inserted temporarily to guide the cannula. He then removes the obturator and inserts the inner cannula into the outer cannula. This can be removed periodically for cleaning mucus.

"All done, breathing seems easier and normal now," Tom exclaims while wiping away some blood.

"Ok, we'll have to keep a close watch on the mucus buildup if any and empty the inner cannula."

"Way to go doc!" Rusty shouts as he beams at Tom.

"You missed your calling," Jerome adds.

"Ok guys, all part of a day's work."

A top priority has been placed on the Korean People's Navy (KPN) bases on the Yellow Sea side to locate the enemy submarine and destroy it. Four hours has elapsed and the North Korean Romeo submarine out of Nampo is almost to the rendezvous point to provide reconnaissance for follow up vessels out of the Haeju Navy base which is farther south.

The North Koreans are not aware that the Richmond has located the oil rig and is now positioned there after a short one hour run from the rendezvous point. Haeju is located 125 miles from the rendezvous point so their vessels, a helo carrying Nampo design FFH light frigate with SS-N-2 STYX cruise missiles , 2-30mm Gatling guns, and 4 RBU 1200 ASW deck launched rockets, and another Romeo submarine, are in route, but to intercept the Richmond, they change course and travel due West assuming their enemy is heading South to escape.

Nampo Frigate Design from Krivak I Class
Public Domain Image

They have also been steaming for 4 hours so they are 60 miles west of Haeju. Another 30 miles and they will be due south of the rendezvous point to block any exit attempt.

Sonar searches are limited to 25 miles due to transmission loss which varies with sonar operation frequencies that lie between 500 hz and 8 khz. So both the recon Romeo and the other pursuing vessels have not observed sonar tonals from the Richmond. And there's no chance for a convergence zone where sonar waves deflect upwards and reflect off of the surface to extend the range – it just isn't deep enough.

The recon Romeo turns South from the rendezvous point and passes within 4 miles of the oil rig. Six hours have now elapsed and the frigate and escorting Romeo turn North about 60 miles due South of the oil rig. The

Seal submersible is still 2 hours away from the rendezvous point.

The USS Richmond forward spherical search array (LAB) is in a passive mode and observes the recon Romeo by its active sonar search mode. Captain Culver is now the conning officer with Mr. Slater as fire control officer.

"Torpedo room, fire control, make tube 1 and 2 ready and open outer doors."

"Fire control, torpedo room, tubes 1 and 2 ready, outer doors open."

The BSY-1 operator applies the TMA target motion analyzer program to the recon Romeo target now called Master 1. The calculation determines the angle on the bow (the position of the enemy with respect to the sub), the target speed, range, and target bearing. These numbers were reported to the Captain.

"Sonar, conn, stand by," orders Captain Culver.

"Conn, sonar, standing by."

"Match sonar bearings and shoot tube 1 and 2, Master 1."

"Match sonar bearings and shoot tube 1 and 2, Master 1, aye."

The large pistons of the ejection pumps drives the Mk 48 AD torpedoes out of their tubes while the Otto fuel engine comes up to speed.

"Tubes 1 and 2 fired electrically," the combat officer reports.

"Very well."

"Conn, sonar, torpedoes running normal and clear."

"Acknowledged," the Captain replies.

The Mk 48 AD torpedoes come up to 50 knots (57.5mph) quickly while drawing out the tethered command wire.

"What's the time to contact, Mr. Slater?"

"Four minutes and 12 seconds sir."

"Conn, sonar, unit one has acquired, unit two has acquired sir."

"Cut the wire, shut outer doors, reload tubes 1 and 2." The Captain orders.

The Mk48 AD torpedoes were in their homing attitude, relentless and noted for not being distracted by decoys. The recon Romeo sonar immediately detected the approaching weapons and the sub started to zigzag out of desperation.

"Conn, sonar, two explosions bearing one one ze-ro, range 7,031 yards."

"Sonar, conn, well done, pass the word."

"Aye sir."

"Mr. Slater we may be now exposed. The enemy's ships and submarines may have had some indication of the explosion so we can't wait. We'll proceed to meet the submersible."

"Very well sir."

"Helm, conn, set course to bearing ze-ro six ze-ro, set flank speed."

Conn, helm, coming to bearing ze-ro six ze-ro, flank speed, aye."

"Helm, conn come to periscope depth."

"Conn, helm, come to periscope depth, aye."

"Hopefully Mr. Slater, the Seals have their antennas up now as they approach rendezvous. They are one hour away. Get their position and set our bearing. We will come to them for pickup."

"Yes sir."

On Board the DCS

"Jerome, I'm getting a signal," Rusty says with a little excitement.

"DCS, DCS, this is Richmond. Give us your position and heading."

"Richmond, 15 miles out, heading two four ze-ro."

"DCS, DCS, maintain heading, we will announce our position every mile, be prepared to come aboard."

"Richmond, aye, be prepared for casualty- two gunshot wounds."

"DCS, will do."

The two vessels approach until the Richmond slows down to a halt. Then the Seals maneuver the submersible behind the submarine and wait until the Richmond crew opens the DDS door and stands by with tether lines. Jerome activates the Rendezvous and Docking System. Guide lights on the DDS help visibility as Jerome slows down and smoothly enters his nose into the doorway. He stops and the crew positions their tether lines and then waves him to continue entry. He slowly powers the propeller to ease completely in to the dry dock. The front hatch is closed, the crew returns inside, and the Seals begin to enter the after hatch while Captain Culver remains concerned about the 98 feet of water.

"Chief, we need an upper body sling for Jack," Tom announces. They ease Jack down inside and he is immediately taken to sick bay where the medics check vital signs, then start a glucose IV and antibiotic. They will remove the bandages, clean the wounds, and redress the hip wound after removing the bullet, but reserve judgement on the facial damage. The other Seals come below, get a warm welcome, a long shower (despite the normal limits), then steak, potatoes, green beans, biscuits and apple pie. They're back!

"Captain, I'd like to go down to sick bay and talk to the Chief Medic about Chief Cody's wounds – can he tolerate additional time or should he be evacuated as soon as possible."

"Good idea, Mr. Slater, we need to take the best course of action when we can but unfortunately based on our tactical situation."

"Thank you sir."

Sick Bay

"Chief, can you give me a heads up on Jack Cody?"

"Yes sir, ideally, these types of injuries should be addressed within 8 hours but considering the circumstances we'll have to loosely accomplish the healing procedures for revisions to occur later."

"We must maintain the airway, control any hemorrhaging, and keep him stable. Then we will irrigate the facial wounds with isotonic sodium chloride, then perform a debridement of the affected areas – that is excise any destroyed or wasted tissue. After that, leave the area open to close naturally – called healing by secondary intention with scar revision later. We'll have to close the inner layers with absorbable 4-0 or 5-0 sutures to hold the muscles. But the best thing we can do is to get him into plastic surgery as soon as possible, he'll have to have his jaw and chin rebuilt with new teeth implants and skin grafts on the nose"

"Thank you Chief, I'll pass it on to the Captain for his consideration."

"Mr. Slater, we have but one choice now, we've got to face the enemy head on, there's no where to hide and our provisions won't last much longer."

"Yes sir, what's the course of action?"

"Remove Mk48 AD torpedoes from tubes 1 and 2. Load two UGM-84 Harpoons in tubes 1 and 2. Set course due South, we'll run into whatever's down there and fight our way out of the Yellow Sea."

"Aye Captain."

"Helm, conn, set course bearing 1 8 ze-ro, speed 2/3 standard."

"Conn, helm, course bearing 1 8 ze-ro, speed 2/3 standard, aye."

"Mr. Slater, keep our LAB spherical array in passive mode, I'm sure the North Koreans are blasting the area with their sonars."

"I agree sir."

1 Hour Later

Harpoon UGM - 84
Public Domain Image

"Conn, sonar, enemy sonar is focused on our position."

"Sonar, conn, what bearings?"

"Conn, sonar, contact bearing 1 9 ze-ro, Master 2, either Kilo destroyer or light Nampo class frigate."

"Sonar, conn, acknowledged."

"Mr. Slater, whether the surface vessel is a destroyer or a frigate, either one carries helicopters. What is our distance?"

"We calculate 26.8 miles sir."

"Very well, delay no longer, launch Harpoons."

"Yes, sir."

The UGM-84 missiles were encased in buoyant capsules for proper placement in the torpedo tube. They were especially programmed to perform a 'pop-up' maneuver before attacking the ship to confuse an antimissile system that may be onboard and active.

"Firing point procedures, tubes one and two, Master 2."

"Conn, fire control, TMA solution complete."

"Sonar, conn, stand by."

"Conn, sonar, standing by, aye."

"Match sonar bearings and shoot tubes 1 and 2, Master 2."

"Match sonar bearings and shoot tubes 1 and 2, Master 2, aye."

"Conn, sonar, rocket booster ignited."

"Sonar, conn, report target acquisition."

"Conn, sonar, report target acquisition, aye."

The missiles had jettisoned their cannisters, unfolded the wings and fins, and were now flying near the speed of sound at sea level to avoid radar contact. After 3 minutes the missile radar seeker turned on and the Harpoons homed in on their target.

"Conn, sonar, target acquired."

"Sonar, conn, well done."

The Harpoons then executed their pop-up maneuver and slammed into the frigate. One explosion, then another seconds later, were observed by sonar. One hit on the bow of the frigate and placed a gaping hole on the starboard side at the water line. The other occurred aft of the bridge, destroyed the RBU torpedo launcher and made a hole in the deck down to the crew quarters. The ship started to list to starboard by the bow as fire erupted near the stern.

"Conn, sonar, Romeo Master 3 is surfacing."

"Sonar, conn, maintain contact."

Mr. Slater, the Romeo must have surfaced to pick up survivors. Let's take advantage, proceed to flank speed and circumvent the area."

"Very well, sir."

"Helm, conn, proceed to flank speed, bearing 1 5 zero."

"Conn, helm, proceed to flank speed, bearing 1 5 zero, aye."

"Mr. Slater, let's reload tubes 1 and 2 with Mk 48 AD torpedoes, I don't think we'll need Harpoons once we're in deep water."

"Torpedo room, conn, reload tubes 1 and 2 with Mk 48 AD torpedoes."

"Conn, torpedo room, load tubes 1 and 2 with Mk 48 AD torpedoes, aye."

At periscope depth, the unobserved USS Richmond rounded the damaged ship that was now listing at forty degrees while the Romeo submarine picked up survivors in a rubber raft. Other crew members were swimming away from the burning oil covered water toward the submarine. Mr. Slater announced that they were entering the Yellow Sea and would soon be in deeper water. Captain Culver headed toward his stateroom. Now to take care of Chief Cody, he mumbled to himself.

Chief's Quarters

"Chief Parker, I'm here to return your feather, it was heap big medicine," Tom says thankfully.

"Welcome back Tom, heard you were in a tight spot."

"Yeah, it comes with the territory, I'm counting my blessings."

"Well, our Great Spirit was watching over you, the feather was indeed big medicine. You've earned it. Keep it to show your children – it will bring honors around the campfires."

"Thanks Chief, you're ok!"

At the Conn

Lt. Stuart was serving as OOD when Commander Slater said to contact Seoul for helicopter assistance to summon Chief Cody for immediate transportation to Walter Reed Hospital at Bethesda Maryland.

"Sir, I'll send an encrypted message over the floating wire antenna to Satellite. The SS SSIX system can forward it to Seoul. What coordinates and ETA should I specify?"

"Very well, Latitude 37.3684 and Longitude 124.6073. ETA at 0145. Have them contact the USS Richmond upon arrival to begin surface procedures."

Down below, the medical officer changed Jack's bandages, cleaned the wounds, and informed him of the transfer. Jack was coherent but unable to speak so he looked at the Chief and blinked his eyes. The Chief seemed to sense an attempt to express thanks when Jack raised his arm and shook his hand.

The USS Freedom Littoral Combat ship was cruising the shallow water near Inchon, South Korea, when a message arrived to prepare the Seahawk MH-60 R helicopter for pickup of a wounded Seal on board the USS Richmond.

The Freedom LCS-1 was a shallow water minesweeper and ASW ship with angular designs of the hull and superstructure for some stealth capability. Her main mission was to provide defense against small boats that come down below the DMZ line to eavesdrop on telecommunications. Tens of thousands of North Korean trained hackers are engaged in the disruption of banking transfers and computer operations in order to demand ransom for the restoration of the systems. Over 150 countries are affected by these cyberattacks and the attempt to conceal computer activity from the enemy has been weak.

The Skyhawk lifted off at 0130 and headed toward the coordinates. Upon arrival, the pilot contacted the Richmond over the VHF channels.

"USS Richmond, this is Skyhawk. Request permission to standby for pickup of wounded seaman."

"Skyhawk, USS Richmond, permission granted. Will now surface to make transfer."

The Richmond was at periscope depth with the towed array fully deployed, Captain Culver wanted to eavesdrop on anything that made noise. She soon nosed up and broke through the surface. Water washed over the sail and bow as she rose quickly since the ballast tanks were being emptied by high pressure air.

The Skyhawk moved over with landing lights to hover about 20 feet above the forward deck as the hatch opened and Jack was placed into the carriage bed. It slowly rose up to the helicopter where it was lifted inside. Immediately, the Skyhawk circled to the right and disappeared. The Richmond slowly descended back to periscope depth and proceeded south.

"Sonar, conn, any tonals observed?"

"Conn, sonar, nothing except a few fish when we increase sensitivity."

"Very well."

Waiting in Seoul was the Gulfstream 111 NI73 PA Air Ambulance of Phoenix Air. Contracted by DOD for special ambulatory service, the intercontinental service provider had a complete medical facility with staff. Jack was swept aboard and the twin jet engine was soon airborne with a cruising speed of 508 mph. It would refuel in San Diego then proceed to Bethesda Naval Hospital.

Next Day

Commander Slater entered the command area to begin his watch when he saw Captain Culver.

"Good morning sir," he cheerfully said.

"Good morning Bill," the Captain replied.

It felt good not to be so formal for a change and Mr. Slater took advantage without being obtrusive.

"Sir, I noticed you studying the charts, have you a plan?"

"Well, I've been thinking, we've completed our mission and we do have the liberty to be aggressive with North Korea, militarily of course."

"What do you have in mind?"

"I'd like to hit the Sinpo South Shipyard and take out the ballistic missile submarine that's under construction."

"With all due respect sir, a strike by us from here would require a trajectory across the entire country. Their air defenses could stop it cold."

"Maybe not if we launched 6 Tomahawks in unison or as close as possible. One might get through."

"Yes it might. What's the range."

"From our coordinates yesterday I calculate 307 miles – direct line of flight. It's located on the east coast north of Hamhung. But we better check with Pearl Harbor before we proceed, send a message to PACFLT and explain our situation."

"Immediately sir,"

Nimitz-MacArthur Headquarters / Pearl Harbor

Upon receipt of the encrypted satellite message from the USS Richmond, the general staff met with the COMPACFLT commander to consider the request to strike the Sanpo South Shipyard.

The Adjacent opens with the comment, "Gentlemen, we must consider this request immediately before the Richmond is out of the range of the Tomahawk target. Soon she will be in the South China Sea to continue to avoid enemy pursuit. On the East side of North Korea, the Sea of Japan has heavy submarine and surface traffic making it difficult to strike from that side."

"What's the status of the ballistic missile submarine program?" One of the officers asks.

"The 38 North study group has satellite imagery of the Sinpo South Shipyard activity. There seems to be an aggressive schedule to build and deploy the SLBM. Continuous movement of parts occurs, sections of the submarine's pressure hull can be seen, and a service tower is holding a launch cannister support near the missile test stand for ejection testing. Also, a submersible missile test stand and submarine are at the same berth. Construction halls and a gantry crane are in the vicinity while construction of an L shaped pier is near complete. The finished product will be called a SINPO-C BMS.

"What's the proof that it'll be a BMS?" Another officer asks.

"Yes, well the beam width of the pressure hull sections is greater then the width for a Romeo class submarine. The greater width will accommodate the launch tubes of the missiles, so it must be a SINPO-C."

The commander speaks, "We don't know what the political fallout of the drone attack will be, it could go either way, an attempt to form a humane government or a last ditch effort to create this weapon as blackmail. Since the Richmond is in position to attempt to solve this problem, I say go ahead. Tell them to strike!"

Lt. Stuart comes to the Captain's stateroom, knocks on the door, and stands at attention.

"Sir, a Priority message just arrived on the VHF antenna receiver. It's a one word message – 'Proceed'."

Tomahawk TLAM-E
Public Domain Image

"Thank you, tell Mr. Slater to set the missile launch stations."

"Yes sir."

The RGM/UGM – 109 E was the latest version of the Block IV Tomahawk missile – the TLAM -E. It has a 1000 pound warhead, range 900 nautical miles, and speed of 546 miles per hour at tree top level. The operating system includes the Theatre Mission Planning Center (TMPC), Afloat Planning System, and the Combat Control System (CCS), exclusive for submarines.

Improvements over earlier versions of the missile include updates in the navigation system and guidance computers and the anti-jam GPS. If re-targeting is needed, two way satellite communication is available for inflight navigation changes.

The small missile cross-section at low altitudes

makes radar detection difficult and the turbofan engine low heat emission affects infrared detection.

The terrain contour watching (TERCOM) radar guidance system compares stored map references to observed land marks while in flight. The optical digital matching system (DSMAC) compliments the other by comparing terrain images against stored terrain images.

"Man battle station, missile," Mr. Slater announces over the 1 MC intercom.

"Helm, conn, come to missile launch depth."

"Conn, helm, come to missile launch depth, aye."

"Combat system, conn, report prelaunch phase."

"Conn, combat system, weapon power on, guidance initialized, target data loaded."

"Combat system, conn, report launch phase."

"Conn, combat system, Intent to launch signal (ITL) activated, missile battery on, ship power off, missile enable signal on, target select complete."

"Firing point procedures, THAM-E tubes one through six," the Captain orders.

The combat system officer then inserts the launch key and presses the firing switch while the "Six shooter" hatch opens hydraulically. The first TLAM-E then burst upward through the plastic of the loading cannister with high pressure air and climbed the 30 feet to the surface. Four seconds later, the rocket motor ignited as the missile crossed through the surface and climbed a few feet above the water. Fourteen seconds later, the rocket motor jettisoned and the turbofan engine started to accelerate the missile to its 546 miles per hour cruising speed as it turned down and proceeded to level flight.

Immediately after jettisoning the rocket motor, the second missile was launched followed by the remaining four missiles in sequence.

The GPS, TERCOM, and DSMAC then took command guiding the missiles to the preplanned target as the open hatch backfilled with water to compensate for weight loss. The missile VLS interlock circuit disengaged and the hatch closed.

"Mr.Slater, proceed to flank speed, set altitude to 150 feet, and retrieve the towed TB-23 array. Activate the LAB bow and conformal arrays."

"Yes, sir."

The depth of water as they ventured off the South Korean coast was 230 feet, allowing much needed and desired maneuverability.

"Mr. Slater, when you get a moment come to my stateroom, I'd like your opinion on something."

"Yes sir, first chance."

The OOD was somewhat puzzled by the request, there certainly weren't any technical issues with the ship.

"What do you think are the chances of the Tomahawks being successful?"

"That's a tough question sir, look at their defense. The North Koreans have the old Russian version of the Sam missile sights. The SA- 2,3,and 5 systems have a range from 25 to 300 meters and are supported by early warning radar. They have complete aerial coverage but a little weak around the DMZ where our Tomahawks flight plan takes place. Most are concentrated around Pyongyang.

Then there's the MANPADs, numerous shoulder weapons and the thousands of 23 to 57 mm antiaircraft artillery batteries. Finally, the Krawdrat – M mobile air defense with three missiles on a turntable. I do think the Tomahawks could get through though at low altitude."

"Yes, but how about the new KN-06 state of the art system. Phased array radar that can engage 4 targets at the same time. It's a copy of the Russian S-300 that has self-learning software to analyze every weapon it encounters. It's been said that the system has taken out warheads traveling at 5km per second at a distance of 30 km. And the Russians claim that it can knock out our Tomahawks. These systems had their eye on our cruise missiles in Syria and could lockup but the Russians did not want to expand the conflict."

"Yes sir, but I find that a little hard to believe. I do know that the North Koreans don't have many of them yet."

"I hope so, we need to get at least two of the six through the gauntlet."

Maximum speed was maintained until they reached the East China Sea. Then speed was reduced to 2/3 standard and the ship brought to periscope depth with the TB-23 towed array deployed in a 'short stay' for quick retrieval if threatened. The captain was still concerned that the rocket noise made by the launching Tomahawks had been observed by enemy forces.

"Helm, conn, come to 4 knots speed."

"Conn, helm, 4 knots speed, aye."

"Mr. Slater, let's take a look around. Swing the periscope 360 degrees if you will."

"Yes sir."

Thanks to the classified research lab at Manassas, Virginia, known as "Area 51 of the Navy', a thirty dollar militarized X Box controller had been incorporated into the periscope system for ease of operation.

"No visual contacts Captain," the OOD replies.

"Very well. Sonar, conn, any tonals observed?"

"Conn, sonar, no sir."

"Sonar, conn, any acoustic response on the array hydrophones?"

"Conn, sonar, no sir, noise level minus 60 db."

"Helm, conn, what's our position and depth?"

"Conn, sonar, Latitude 27.0904, Longitude 126.2126, Depth 3,400 feet."

"Helm, conn, what's our range and bearing to Okinawa?"

"Conn, helm, Range, 131 miles, Bearing 118 degrees."

"Mr. Slater, contact White Beach Port Facilities at Katsuren and request anchorage and pier service. This crew needs liberty."

"Very good, sir."

"Sonar, radio, conn, proceeding to White Beach Port Facility. Contact the Awase Transmitter Facility for permission to berth and anchor at the base."

"Conn, radio, contact Awase Transmitter Facility, aye."

This Navy port was located at the tip of Katsuren

Peninsula on the Pacific Ocean side with two piers and anchorage to provide facilities and services for nuclear ships and submarines of the 7th Fleet that make frequent calls. It is primarily known as an amphibious center for Marines and has ample accommodations for liberty – cabins, sailboats, jet skies, and picnic areas.

"Conn, radio, the Fleet Activity Commander has approved your request for entry with temporary anchorage until an opening occurs at one of the piers at 1400."

"Very well, helm, conn, proceed bearing 118 degrees, speed 2/3 standard."

"Conn, helm, bearing 118 degrees, speed 2/3 standard, aye."

1 Hour Later

"Conn, sonar, temporary contact at 60 mile convergence zone, bearing 332 degrees."

"Sonar, conn, maintain LAB and conformal arrays . Report any acoustic or tonal response."

"Conn, sonar, report any acoustic or tonal response, aye."

In deep water, an isothermal layer that has the speed of sound increasing with depth (positive gradient), can have signals deflect back up to the surface before they reach bottom, providing there is a minimum of 200 feet between the curving signal and the bottom. This phenomenon results in a convergence zone of combined signals at the surface thirty miles out. It can provide temporary recognition of hostiles there. A second convergence zone at 60 miles can also be effective enhancing the range of sonar coverage.

"Mr. Slater, I think we've been discovered or at least the enemy knows our bearing and is following us. Yet he's maintaining a distance until we've reached deep water. Then he'll make his move and not leave a trace of us here which makes me think he's Chinese. I am going to assume that he will now close the gap. Our surveillance so far has not shown any activity other than surface traffic."

"Yes sir, I suggest we runout the SSXBT bathythermograph and check for a thermal layer that we can position under to observe the contact without being noticed."

"Ok, let me know what you find and we'll set the altitude. Also, have sonar calculate his speed if he shows again. That'll tell us the class of boat that we're dealing with."

"Right away, sir."

Thirty-six minutes later

"Conn, sonar, temporary contact at 30 mile convergence zone."

"Sonar, conn, what is his speed?"

"Conn, sonar, 40 miles per hour."

"Sonar, conn, maintain active sonar."

"Conn, sonar, maintain active sonar, aye."

"Mr. Slater, he's on our trail and will be here soon.

At his speed he must be the new Chinese Jin class boat. Keep sonar active while we're under this thermal layer. Maybe we'll see him before he notices us."

"Helm, conn, left full rudder, ahead 1/3 standard until bearing 332 degrees. Then all stop."

"Conn, helm, left full rudder, ahead 1/3 standard until bearing 332 degrees, then full stop, aye."

"Mr. Slater, we'll meet him head on."

"Yes, sir."

"Torpedo room, fire control, tubes 1,2,3,4 ready, outer doors open."

"Fire control, torpedo room, tubes 1,2,3,4 ready, outer doors open, aye."

"Sonar, conn, report tonals and acoustic response."

"Conn, sonar, no activity, tonal and acoustic."

The closing enemy was the latest Chinese class attack submarine, the Jin class, type 095, with a reduced acoustic signature, a more advanced nuclear reactor, an active/passive flank array sonar, and a hi/lo frequency towed array. An innovating feature was the introduction of a "cabin-raft" shock absorber deck to reduce noise levels by 35 db.

She carries the YU-6 torpedo similar to the MK48, thanks to another reverse engineering program and the JL-2 ballistic missile. But most significant is the "shaftless rim-driven pumpjet" silent propulsion system.

Instead of a propellor shaft, fan blades are attached to a rotating cylindrical band that is the rotor for the electrical motor. The housing is the motor stator with the electro-magnetic forces to cause rotation of the blades -extremely low noise. Two of these pumpjets are built into shrouds on the stern.

"Chief of the watch, rig ship for depth charge (torpedo)."

"Aye aye, sir," Chief Parker responds.

"Mr. Slater, we should at least hear her reactor coolant pumps or propeller noise soon if her sonar is passive which I would doubt. I wonder if that boat has the new pumpjet concept. Either way, be prepared for a quick response."

"Yes, sir."

"Conn, sonar, torpedo launch, range 44,000 yards (25 miles), speed accelerating to 200 knots (230 miles per hour). ETA 6.5 minutes."

"Sonar, conn, acknowledged."

**Supercavitating Torpedo
Public Domain Image**

"Torpedo room, fire control, match sonar bearings and snap shot tubes 1 and 2, Master 4."

"Fire control, torpedo room, sonar bearings matched, snap shot tubes 1 and 2, Master 4, aye."

"Tubes 1 and 2 fired electrically," reports the fire control officer. There wasn't time for the TMA target motion analyzer to determine the target operating status.

"Conn, sonar, torpedoes running normal on bearing

332 degrees."

"Sonar, conn, very well, report closing times with approaching torpedo."

"Conn, sonar, reporting closing times with torpedo."

The high speed enemy torpedo was the new supercavitating design that created a tear drop shaped bubble to completely surround the weapon with gas and air for high velocity travel without the friction of water. Powered by a rocket engine, the exhaust of which was released at the front of the torpedo to form the bubble.

A Russian design, the export version was labeled the Shkval-E and it had a published range of 9.3 miles although this version must have a larger rocket engine in order to travel 25 miles. Being very noisy from the rocket exhaust and high cavitation, the design is quite vulnerable to being locked on by an adversary.

The Mk 48 AD launch has now required 2 minutes to execute which reduces the arrival time of the enemy weapon to 4.5 minutes. At the speed of 63 miles per hour (1.05 miles per minute), the Mk 48 will intercept the torpedo after 3.55 minutes at a distance of 3.73 miles from the Richmond.

"Conn, sonar, two explosions , range 6565 yards."

"Sonar, conn, acknowledged, give me a debris field status."

"Conn, sonar, debris field clear at bearing 332."

"Sonar, conn, very well."

"Chief of the watch, conn, damage control report."

"Conn, all antenna, sonar, and array systems functional," Chief Parker reports.

The huge explosion in the line of sight of the Richmond has convinced the enemy submarine that the Richmond has been sunk and it continues on course at the position now of 22.6 miles from the Richmond.

"Torpedo room, fire control, set TMA and launch tubes 3 and 4, Master 5."

"Fire control, torpedo room, match sonar bearing and shoot tubes 3 and 4, Master 5."

The ejection pump drives the torpedoes clear of the tubes as the guidance tethers follow until the homing mode triggers and the tethers are severed. Immediately the enemy observes the attack and releases chaff along with acoustic countermeasures while turning north to escape the assault. A long run begins to occur with the 63 mile per hour torpedoes pursuing the 40 mile per hour submarine. An eventual explosion at 62.5 miles from the action would happen as the torpedoes catch up but they will run out of Otto fuel after their limit of 24 miles. The Chinese submarine will survive for another day but the noisy fast supercavitating torpedo has a lot of modifications needed to become a viable weapon.

"Mr. Slater, proceed to periscope depth, if all clear, prepare to surface. Inform Katsuren of our late arrival and confirm our berthing arrangement."

"Yes, sir."

Later, after coming to the surface and proceeding on bearing 118 to the White Beach Naval Facility, a response to the radio message arrives.

"Conn, radio, the Fleet Activity Commander sends

his congratulations on the mission and welcomes your ship. His transcript is as follows:

Prepared for your arrival. Sent an all points Immediate priority 'Submiss' message to air and sea rescue teams upon receiving reports by ASW aircraft of an explosion in the vicinity of your position. Will rescind the message and debrief the situation when you arrive. Congratulations on your success and safe return,"

"Radio, conn, message received."

White Beach Officer's Lounge

Captain Culver is reading the top story in the Washington Times. Headlines described the attack at Pyongyang that killed North Korean top brass but what struck him was the news of the four Tomahawk missiles that destroyed the Ballistic Missile Submarine that was under construction plus part of the Sanyo South Shipyard. He was waiting for a detailed classified briefing at Pearl Harbor and wondered at the ability of the media to sniff out stories when his thoughts were interrupted.

"Captain, Chief Parker would like a word with you."

"Very well, bring him in."

The Chief enters and salutes.

"At ease Chief, what's up?"

"Sir during our routine maintenance procedures I noticed that the starboard retrievable bow plane seemed to drag during operation. I'd like to look at the hydraulic cylinders and see if replacement is needed."

"Is that necessary now?"

"Well sir, the planes do operate independently but when in unison that plane would follow the port bow plane and make it cumbersome to maintain a level platform."

"How much time do you need?"

"Three days sir."

"All right. I'll extend liberty after we load provisions."

"Thank you sir," the Chief added as he saluted and left.

Chief's Quarters

Jerome and Rusty went to Tom to offer a suggestion.

"Tom, we've managed to catch a ride on the E3 Sentry that's going over to Elmendorf Air Base for an upgrade on the AWACS system. Would you be interested in joining us since we're here for three days before returning to Pearl."

"Sure, let's check with Mr. Slater, when does it leave?"

"Tomorrow morning at 0700."

Commander Slater's Office

After explaining the available flight, they address the OOD.

"Sir, we have this opportunity and would like to

take advantage of it if you approve."

"Yes of course, I'll finish your fitness reports and issue travel orders."

That evening Captain Culver entered the Chief's Quarters and bid farewell to the men. He shook hands and thanked them for an outstanding effort. He also said that he would like an update on Jack Cody when they return to Norfolk. The next morning Chief Parker went with them to Kadena Air base that is home for the largest Air Force Wing – the 18th Wing. He bid them good luck while Tom thanked him for his support and kindness. He watched as the four engine Sentry with the rotating disc on top that served as the radar dome lifted off and headed east.

Three Days Later

The USS Richmond is to depart at 0830. Captain Culver and Commander Slater are standing on the sail as the deck crew prepares to cast off. Just before 0800 a bugle call is heard then a bell is struck eight times. A Navy band strikes up the National Anthem and the commanding officers with the crew come to attention and salute while the flag is raised. When the colors are secured, a second bugle is heard and then silence. Captain Culver turns toward his executive officer and says, "Mr. Slater, let's go home!!"

> Author's Note: When the speed of sound decreases with depth (negative gradient), the signals will bend down toward the bottom and not create a convergence.

CHAPTER FIVE

"We Have Met the Enemy and They are Ours"

Virginia Beach

Mary and the girls were waiting at the Naval Air Station Oceana for Tom's flight to arrive. It's been three months since he left and she had not heard a word until he called from Elmendorf Air Base yesterday.

As usual, she never knew if he was alive or where and what his mission would require of him. She did know that his missions contributed to the safety and security of his country and she made herself willing to accept that with nothing more.

It was January and blustery with snow flurries as he stepped out of the C37A Gulfstream and ran across the tarmac to the terminal. The girls ran to meet him and hugged his legs as he reached out to Mary. She tried to hide her tears while he embraced and kissed her.

"Let's hurry home everyone, and get out of this freezing weather."

They piled into the car and merged into the slow moving traffic as the roads were beginning to get a dusting. It was great to be back at Virginia Beach and Tom hurriedly unloaded when they arrived and settled down in his recliner. While unpacking his overnight bag, Mary noticed something unusual. It was a beautiful feather in a plastic bag.

"What's this Tom, a souvenir?"

"You might say that, the Chief of the Boat was full blooded Indian and a great guy. He gave me that to have protection and blessings from the Great Spirit."

"Isn't that a bit superstitious?"

"No, not at all, that feather goes back generations to a great Chief and I'm honored to have it. I'm going to frame it and hang it in my study."

"Boy, it must be important," Mary replies while holding it up into the light.

Later, after everyone has settled down, Mary asks how Jack Cody was doing. She had received a Christmas card from Pat.

"Well, Mary, he's ok but he was wounded. He's recovering at Bethesda. I promised that I would go up to see him as often as I could."

"Oh, how serious is it.?"

"Facial injury, and a hip wound but not life threatening. He will need repeated surgeries though."

"Oh, I'm so sorry."

"He's ok – great attitude, a tough guy."

"Should I contact his wife?"

"I'd let him do it that's their business."

"You're right. I would like to go with you sometime."

"Sure thing."

Bethesda Naval Hospital

As Tom entered the room, Jack was standing by the window supported by a cane. The right side of his face was covered with bandage but he was breathing freely.

Bethesda Naval Hospital
Public Domain Image

Tom tossed some new magazines on the bed and said,

"Hey, you're looking good Jack, how do you feel," while shaking hands.

Jack reached down for a pad and wrote, "Great, and I'm walking pretty good."

"How many surgeries have you had?"

Again the pad, "Six so far, but I've got a long way to go. They did straighten out my septum though, it's good to be able to breathe again."

While trying to be discrete, Tom continues, "Had any visitors." He was curious about the departure of Pat and was hopeful that they would be reunited.

Jack writes, "A few, my folks, a couple of Seal Team buddies, an officer from Naval Special Warfare Command (NSWC), and a local pastor -and now you."

"Well, I'll hop up here every couple of weeks unless I get deployed. How are you being fed?"

Slowly writing this time, he says, "Liquids with a straw and an occasional IV. Can't wait for a hamburger and a pizza."

"I want to be here when that happens. Look I better hit the trail. You take care and stop chasing those nurses."

"Ha, don't be a stranger!!"

As he walked out, Tom sensed that Jack missed his wife and thought that his mate was putting up a good front.

Pearl Harbor

The USS Richmond would under go a mini-refit while the reactor was shut down and shore power was applied. Reactor coolant water would be recycled through the subtender massive ion beds for purity and then returned to the boat. Spent Tomahawk cannisters from the launch tubes would be dispersed and the six-gun shooter launch tubes reloaded. Torpedoes and acoustic countermeasures would be loaded while operational tests would be performed on all systems.

A major effort would be the assimilation of records. Logs, data sheets for sonar and radio, and ESM reports would be forwarded for evaluation by PACFLT. In addition, a 200 page report titled "Patrol Report of Richmond" was to be submitted. It was compiled 4 times daily by the off-going OOD and JOOD.

On one of the rare occasions when some leisure time was available, Captain Culver and Commander Slater sat down in the officer's lounge for a break from the mundane activity.

Their discussion about the mission brought up an interesting point regarding propulsion.

"You know Bill, that Chinese sub wasn't observed by our TB-23 hydrophones. It was extremely quiet acoustically."

"Yes, the sonar convergence zone is what helped us observe him. Of course he wasn't holding back during the attack, blasting us with active sonar."

"That rim-drive pumpjet is really good with electrical forces driving the blades instead of a shaft," the Captain adds.

"Well sir, remember that movie Hunt for Red October? It took the technology one step further – no moving parts. The magnetohydrodynamic drive (MHD) propelled the ship using only electric and magnetic fields. The water is electrified and then directed by the magnetic field to push the vessel. The water is the rotor but travels in a linear direction."

"Yeah, but totally impracticable. The amount of power needed to drive the submarine would be enormous. No, especially the noise generation. Good movie though!"

Captain Culver decides to walk down to the pier for a last look at the Richmond before flying home. While standing on the dock and studying the sail and hull, an elderly lady walks by and stops.

"The ships are beautiful," she says.

"Yes, very streamlined," he adds while trying to be courteous.

"But that one boat," she replies as she points to the Richmond, "the name!"

"The name, what about the name?" he questions.

"With all of the Confederate monuments being taken down, they had to name that one after the capital of the Confederacy – Richmond!"

"Ma'am, if she performs as well as Admiral Buchanan of the Confederate Navy, she'll have a great record."

"Well of all --!!!" the indignant woman responded as she quickly left.

Captain Culver smiled as he thought of his great, great, great grandfather Jerimiah Culver who was given his freedom by Admiral Buchanan. He would remain for the rest of his life as man-servant to his feisty mentor and be with him during his 46 years with the old US Navy where he founded the Naval Academy, then as captain of the Merrimac, and as pursuer of blockaders at Mobile Bay, until finally retirement on the Eastern Shore of Maryland.

He took one last look at the Richmond and turned away to return home to Natchez for a well deserved leave. As he walked along, someone was heard to say that they thought he was whistling Dixie.

North Korea

Peaceful demonstrations have begun to spread across the country. The people have many grievances and now feel compelled to be vocal. With the absence of micromanaging leadership the military stands down, mainly because of their empathy with the suffering public.

A large part of the population has malnutrition and intestinal parasite problems with food and water being diseased and scarce. The government policy of Songun has placed the military as top priority resulting in its being ranked 4th largest in the world. One quarter of the GDP is allocated for military hardware and maintenance of the standing army.

Production is now state controlled rather than being a function of an open economy. The standard guns and butter philosophy is challenged by the "Parallel Development Program". State run enterprises control health, education, housing, and collective farms. Party organs report the people's economic hardship on a daily basis and they have banned any gatherings related to drinking, singing, and other entertainment. Emphasis is placed on the containment of Christmas celebrations although Christmas trees are displayed in Pyongyang but without religious ornaments.

Human rights violations are severe with concentration camps for political prisoners, slave labor, torture, human experimentation, and arbitrary executions. Life is hard in rural areas but not in the showcase capital of Pyongyang.

So the people are taking advantage of this window of opportunity by demonstrating in all the cities and demanding talks with local government leaders, not the Worker's Party leaders nor the Supreme People's

Assembly (SPA) especially the Central People's Committee that is elected by the SPA. The three levels of local government are being contacted; the cities, urban districts, counties and villages. If a consortium of local leaders can be achieved, demands can be made of the ruling party leaders with the implied threat of open rebellion. These demands were easy to derive, just look south of the DMZ border at the South Korea government paradigm.

The Constitution of the Republic of South Korea defines the executive, legislative, and judicial branches. While the executive and legislative branches operate at the national level, the judicial branch operates at both national and local levels. The legislative branch consists of the National Assembly of South Korea with four political parties. The executive branch is led by the elected president who serves one five year term only. The judicial branch has the supreme court, constitutional court, and local courts.

The rigorous education system has resulted in the high technology boom and rapid economic development. It leads the world in consumer electronics. Panels of government officials, scholars, and business leaders planned the production of new materials, robotics, bioengineering, microelectronics, and aerospace with still a steady growth in heavy industry -automobile and ship products.

As the influence of the dissenting population increases, the local leaders begin to listen. The people want to create a representative government with elections and a constitution. The Party leaders finally decide to have discussions with the local leaders and representatives of the demonstrating groups. It is finally agreed upon to consider elections but with outside expertise as consultants. Of course, the best possible source is South Korea.

Some years ago, South Korea created a "Sunshine Policy", a foreign policy regarding North Korea. It specifically stated that no armed provocation by North Korea would be tolerated. South Korea would not absorb North Korea but it would coexist through cooperation and reconciliation. The economic gap would be closed through South Korea business ventures in North Korea. At that time, the negotiations failed to implement an economic plan and the effort ceased. But by using the Sunshine Policy as a benchmark in consideration of the extreme conditions now in North Korea, a successful endeavor will reach fulfillment.

South Korea will introduce manufacturing and research divisions to North Korea. The effort will begin with South Korean management combined with trained North Korean management and workers. Eventually the businesses will merge into a complete North Korean enterprise with part ownership by South Korean minority stockholders.

The North Korean educational system will be invigorated with South Korean teachers and administrative personnel in the fields of technology and medicine while some North Korean students will attend South Korean universities.

The military budget will be reduced with funds reallocated for the building of the infrastructure, especially highways. North Korean nuclear expertise will be redirected to the development of nuclear power stations.

And of course, human rights issues will be addressed.

With a democratic government, manufacturing, education, and reallocation of the GDP, North Korea will become a partner with South Korea and achieve independence.

The people have spoken and the party leaders have now agreed to cooperate on all levels, even to the point of holding elections. North Korea has the potential and if the country makes the effort, a new day will come.

Bethesda Naval Hospital / One Year Later

Tom visits Jack again as he had been doing on a monthly basis. This time he brings Mary along to express her best wishes but also to hear something about Pat.

"How are you progressing Jack," Tom asks.

"Well, actually, I'm leaving next week after 23 operations. I can eat, talk, breathe, and present a reasonable appearance."

"Are you kidding, you're better looking now more than ever."

"Thanks, you beat everything Tom, but I'm very grateful to the dedication and skill of the professionals."

"Well, what's next Jack," Mary asks.

"I'm assigned to recruiting duty for my last year and I'll be starting my ministry studies."

"Way to go Jack," Tom adds "by the way, has Patricia ever come to visit?"

"Yes, one time. It was a stiff formal visit. Neither one of us knew what to say and I couldn't talk. I wrote down a question to ask how well she was doing. She said that she was living with her parents and attending night school for a masters in finance. She doesn't like being a prosecuting attorney. Then of all things, she said that she didn't know why she had come, she was flying in the face of reason. I wrote again that I was going to be doing stateside duty while studying for the ministry and that I still cared. She thanked me and quickly left, I thought emotionally."

Tom speaks up and says, "Here's the letter you gave me to keep."

"And yours is in that drawer over there," Jack adds.

"What's that," Mary asks.

"Oh, just in case something happened."

"Tom, when I get to become attached to some congregation, I want you and your family to visit. I'll let you know."

"Sure thing Jack, we'll be there. Take care," as he leaned over and gave Jack a hug.

Mary also gave him a hug and then they left. As they exited the door Tom glanced at a note that was attached to it. It said, "If you enter this room feeling sorry for my wounds, go somewhere else. These wounds I got in a job I love, while serving the people I love, and protecting the freedom of the country that I love."

North Korea

The former militant nation has now become a republic. It has patterned its government and constitution after that of South Korea and the United States. The economy is booming, people are commuting on the new highways to professional and trade jobs with incomes on a par with South Korea. Collective farming has transformed into independent farms utilizing the latest equipment to enable large scale operations. Health care now covers the entire population and tourism has surprisingly become a big contributor to the GDP.

Improved relations with foreign countries has resulted in new embassies and trade agreements. There are six trillion dollars worth of minerals in the North Korean ground including coal, iron, magnesium, zinc, limestone, graphite, and 2,000 metric tons of gold. Chinese and American mining companies are cooperating with the government to carefully extract the wealth without damaging the environment. The fishing industry in the Sea of Japan and the Yellow Sea is on the increase with new and larger trawlers and processing ships.

North Korea has now become a key player in the Near East and Asian community as well as a positive input to the United Nations. A great addition to the well being and peace of the free world.

The President was expected to deliver this address in January but due to the changing situation in North Korea he decided to hold the session a month later.

At the closing of his address, he announced that the unification of North and South Korea would be official on March 1st.The country would now be called the United Republics of Korea. United States treaties and economic aid would be renegotiated. Most importantly, the American military would be completely withdrawn which included the 35,000 troops from South Korea, the Osan Air Base, the Kunsan Air Base, and the US Fleet in Chinhae. Deployments in Japan, Okinawa, and Guam would remain the same.

Thunderous applause shook the house and lasted for 36 minutes. At the end of the oration, the President called up Captain Culver. As he stood near the Speaker's podium, the President placed the Medal of Honor around his neck and said,

"For conspicuous leadership, gallantry and intrepidity, above and beyond the call of duty, in action against rogue nation forces, and for heroic conduct in the defense and rescue of American personnel, I bestow the nation's highest honor."

Again thunderous applause as Captain Culver looks up into the gallery at members of his crew.

Commander Slater – Distinguished Service Cross

Lieutenant Stuart – Bronze Star

Petty Officer Burns – Silver Star

Chief Jack Cody – Purple Heart, Silver Star

Petty Officer Rusty Draper – Bronze Star with V for Valor

Petty Officer Jerome Black – Bronze Star with V for valor

Chief Parker and crew – Presidential Unit Citation

Later, the Chinese ambassador called upon the President and extended congratulations for the announced withdrawal. Relationships between the two countries would now reach a new level of confidence, trust but still verify.

Muskogee, Oklahoma / Christmas Eve / Two Years Later

The Church was a long, narrow, 19th century style white frame building with a steeple on the pitched roof near the front entrance. Steps would lead up to a small porch with a roof and on each side was a narrow window rounded at the top.

Tom and his family had entered the pleasant surroundings and been ushered to a reserved pew up front. Reverend Cody then made his appearance from a side entrance and said good evening and Merry Christmas.

"I would like to make two announcements today. The first is – let's give a warm welcome to Master Chief Tom Burns, his wife Mary, daughters Sarah and Ava, and now their new son Jack."

The crowded congregation applauded then Jack added quietly, "He saved my life." A sustained pause and murmurs.

"Now my second announcement is very important to our Church. Let me introduce you to our new choir director and financial advisor, my wife Mrs. Cody."

Tom and Mary looked at each other incredulously. How could he have remarried so quick? Then Jack said,

"Come on out Patricia!"

Mary gushed with tears and Tom wiped a tear from his eye. Pat walked over toward Jack and put her arm in his, then gave a small wave to Mary, who waved back.

"Let me begin today with a message for the season. It's a time of giving. Uncle Harry gets a new tie, sister Betty a book, and mother a new robe. But the most important gift to us is the gift of Mary and her child in a manger, -------------------"

As we take leave of this joyous occasion, let us remember the men and women that served our country, military and civilian, and let us remember those men and women that serve now. They could not do more and their sense of duty will not let them do less.

May God Bless Them
and
May God Bless America

AUTHOR'S NOTE

To create a sense of reality, distance calculations were made using Latitude and Longitude coordinates with a multiplier of 69.17 miles per degree. This number is based on the circumference of the equator 24,901 miles, divided by 360 degrees. It does not consider the differences in circumferences at different coordinates due to the spherical shape of the earth but it does provide a reasonable estimate of distance. The complex multiplier based on the actual circumference at Pyongyang would result in distance calculations that were 14.2 percent less than the numbers used in the novel.

The location and time of the collision between the MK 48 and the supercavitating torpedoes were calculated from the closing distance between the torpedoes of 17.3 miles rather than 25 miles because of the 2 minute MK 48 launch delay.

Calculations for the Chinese submarine chase after the torpedo collision were based on the closing distance between submarines at that time of 22.6 miles.

Special thanks to Doug Dombek and Dale Buley for editing the manuscript